D1108402

JELLYBEAN

JELLYBEAN

Tessa Duder

Viking Kestrel

VIKING KESTREL
Published by the Penguin Group
Viking Penguin Inc., 40 West 23rd Street, New York, New York 10010, U.S.A.
Penguin Books Ltd, 27 Wrights Lane, London W8 5TZ England
Penguin Books Australia Ltd, Ringwood, Victoria, Australia
Penguin Books Canada Ltd, 2801 John Street, Markham, Ontario, Canada L3R 1B4
Penguin Books (N.Z.) Ltd, 182-190 Wairau Road, Auckland 10, New Zealand

Penguin Books Ltd, Registered Offices: Harmondsworth, Middlesex, England

First published in New Zealand by Oxford University Press, 1985
First American edition published in 1986
Published simultaneously in Canada

Library of Congress Cataloging in Publication Data
Duder, Tessa. Jellybean.
Originally published: [Auckland] New Zealand: Oxford University Press, 1985.
Summary: The only child of a single mother, Geraldine is tired of having to fit into her mother's busy orchestra schedule, but things begin to change when she discovers a new friend and an ambition to be a conductor.
[1. Single-parent family—Fiction. 2. Mothers—Employment—Fiction.
3. Mothers and daughters—Fiction. 4. Orchestra—Fiction] I. Title
PZ7.D8645Je 1986 [Fic] 86-5553 ISBN 0-670-81235-8

Printed in the United States of America by The Book Press, Brattleboro, Vermont
Set in Bembo
2 3 4 5 6 92 91 90 89 88

Contents

1

The clue is always the cello case, tall and black in its corner of the living-room. When it stays shut, like a masked soldier standing guard over the precious treasure inside, Geraldine knows that there are no big concerts this week. Her mother has finished her daily session of scales and exercises and the cello is now packed away ready for the next school concert, rehearsal, or whatever is on the day's schedule. When the case stays open and empty, and looks like an Egyptian mummy's coffin, Geraldine knows that there is an important concert only a few days away. Then the cello stays out of its case and her mother's practising can be heard at all hours from one end of the flat to the other.

Coming in from school one afternoon in a concert week, Geraldine hears the cello being not so much played, as *worked* at. She knows exactly what she will see as she walks down the creaking hallway towards the living-room: her mother with the golden cello lying against her shoulder, eyes fixed on the music stand, her long dark hair tangled and half over her face, and the cello bow dancing across the strings. As she chews her gingernuts while waiting in the doorway for a break in the music, she recognizes one phrase being played again and again.

Finally her mother's bowing arm drops. She lets out a long breath and looks at Geraldine. She is not smiling. When she is playing she never smiles.

'The Tchaikovsky Fourth. Never a moment's rest.'

There are other names Geraldine has heard her mother use over the years: Brahms, Beethoven, Debussy,

Stravinsky. 'God help me, Richard Strauss,' she once said with something like despair in her voice.

Her mother's eyes return to the music stand. 'Get yourself a drink, Jellybean. I won't be long. Any homework?' she asks, but Geraldine knows that her answer will go unheard. The cello is already singing as she goes back to the kitchen.

It continues to sing while Geraldine wanders out to the back garden to sit on the steps with Quaver, stroking his black fur. She hears the boys over the fence begin their regular afternoon game of soccer and the old man next door trying to start his motor mower. She knows her mother will be furious if he succeeds; she will say she 'can't practise with that racket going on'. But he gives up after several attempts and she hears instead the squeak of the clothes line being twirled around.

There is a cold wind blowing across the yard, making the clothes on their own line dance about. Men's pyjamas and funny long yellowy underpants, she notices, from the flat in the other half of the house. She stands up, still holding Quaver, and returns to the living-room – or studio, as her mother calls it – waiting for the music to finish.

The studio is long and high-ceilinged. Compared with other people's living-rooms, it has an empty feel to it. The floor is just bare wood with a couple of faded oriental rugs. There is a piano, a tall fireplace with flowered tiles down each side, a few chairs, a divan, and a special spotlight shining directly onto the music stand. On a dresser and on shelves along the walls are many books, some pottery plates and vases, two or three paintings, posters advertising concerts, many piles of music, a tape deck, and cassettes arranged in neat rows. Despite the gas fire and a half-hearted beam of late sun through the window, it is nearly as cold inside the house as out.

Today her mother is wearing sheepskin boots and a cardigan which touches the floor on either side of her chair.

Geraldine watches. In all of Rooms Nine and Ten at school, she told her mother recently, there wasn't one single other mother who played the cello in a pub. There wasn't even a mother who played the cello full-stop.

'What do the other mothers do?' her mother asked when she stopped laughing.

'Lots of them work,' Geraldine replied, a little hurt. 'Supermarkets and places. Teachers, stuff like that. A few kids said they don't know what their mothers do all day.'

On several occasions after that, as she sat quietly at the back of the rehearsal hall waiting for her mother to finish packing up the Egyptian coffin, Geraldine realized her remarks were being repeated. '. . . . .the *only* mother who plays the cello in a pub!' she heard clearly. And how they all laughed!

It is true, though. On Tuesdays and Fridays her mother plays at a restaurant place in the city – just short bits of music with a pianist and violinist while people have dinner and drink wine and beer and strange coloured mixtures in long glasses with cherries on top. Then there's the orchestra, of course, and backing at pop concerts, and radio work, and sometimes she goes off to a big theatre every night for three weeks to play for the ballet company, or opera, or a musical show. I know, Geraldine thinks, because I've been there with her. I *know* what my mother does all day – and all night.

The studio is getting colder and colder and still her mother is doing the Tchaikovsky Fourth. Geraldine hugs Quaver closer to her, enjoying the little cat's warmth across her thighs, and wriggles her bottom deep down into the beanchair. The room has grown dark, making the shaft of light onto the music stand brighter. She wonders which baby-sitter will be coming tonight – Leanne, her favourite, who reads her stories and forgets to send her to bed by nine o'clock? Or Karen who turns on the tiny television half-hidden among the books, and who also forgets to send her to bed? Or it may be Veronica who practises the piano very loudly, or Carol who spreads her varsity books over the kitchen table and ignores her completely, or Judith who sends her to bed early so that she can talk on the phone to her boyfriend all night. They are all students of one sort or another. Geraldine is very used to baby-sitters.

Today, a winter Friday, Mum has gone on longer than usual so there must be a very important concert tomorrow night. But she seems at last to have finished the Tchaikovsky Fourth.

'Sorry, Jellybean.' She is holding the cello by the neck and arching her back. 'I had a rehearsal this morning and a radio job after lunch filling in for someone else, so I had to leave my practice until now.'

She pushes up the spike of the cello and stands the instrument with gentle care inside the case. Geraldine has seen this ritual hundreds of times. Now the bow: loosen the knob on the end, and put it in its own slender pocket in the case. Swing the lid shut and the coffin is closed, ready for tonight.

Her mother looks terrible and is rubbing her eyes. She is wearing jeans, a striped shirt and that hairy cardigan Geraldine hates so much. Yet in a short while this weary-looking mother will be ready to go out to the restaurant in her long black skirt, high-necked white blouse, her dark hair untangled and smoothly pinned up: the musician.

'How was school?'

'All right.'

'Anything exciting happen?'

'All the lights went out when it was dark and raining. A girl in my class broke her leg. Mr Gillespie was away. We had another teacher. She got mad at the boys who wouldn't stop talking. The health nurse came to inspect everyone for nits.'

'I hope she didn't find any.'

'Not on me she didn't. Then I had to go to the murder house.'

'Fillings?'

'One.'

'Did it hurt?'

'Yes.' Geraldine thinks further, her tongue feeling the rough edge of the filling. 'I don't feel very well.'

There is a short silence.

'How?'

'There's a pain in the back of my neck. Around the back, there.'

'Do you feel hot?'

'In this room?'

'No, hot inside – shivery, behind your eyes?'

Geraldine shakes her head slowly.

'Sore throat?'

'A bit.' Geraldine swallows cautiously. 'Yes.'

'Do you think it's the injection?'

'I didn't have an injection.'

Another silence. Her mother finishes folding up the music stand and puts it on top of her brief-case of music, ready for tonight.

'I'm sorry, Jellybean, but you know I have to go out to play in town tonight. It's not like you to feel off-colour.'

'I know.' But she didn't say I'm sorry, not for something she couldn't help.

'Leanne is coming to baby-sit. You'll be okay with her. We'll see how you are tomorrow morning.'

Geraldine nods, relieved. Leanne meant a warm bed and a whole night of stories until she fell asleep.

'I'll be back soon after ten. You know that. What do you want for tea?'

'I'm not hungry. Spaghetti on toast.'

'Good, that's easy. All I want, too.'

The phone rings in the kitchen at the other end of the long narrow hall. The telephone stands right next to the stove, so that her mother can stir the pots with one hand and hold the phone with the other while she talks with her friends.

Geraldine sits gloomily in her beanchair, half-reading her book, half-listening to the single 'ding' on the phone as her mother talks, rings up, talks, rings up again. Her voice is too far away to hear clearly what is being said, but Geraldine can hear her own name being mentioned. The room is quite a bit darker when her mother comes back.

'Well, I suppose it had to happen one day. That was Leanne's mother to say she is sick. Flu, like half Auckland. Veronica's going to a youth club, Karen to a film. The others are out.'

'Oh.'

Mum is looking at her watch.

'I'll be all right by myself,' Geraldine says. She thinks, I can sit in my bed and watch the door handle and listen for creaks in the hallway which mean that someone is creeping . . .

'No you won't. Perhaps you can go to . . . .' Geraldine doesn't hear the rest as her mother is already half-way back to the kitchen. More phone calls, then again her mother is in the doorway looking at her watch.

'I'll be all right . . .'

'Jellybean, I can't go out and leave you alone in the flat with a sore throat. Even without a sore throat. It's illegal, apart from anything else. I'd be worrying myself sick through every bit of music.'

Right on, Mum, thinks Geraldine. So would I.

'I've got to leave in half an hour. Oh hell. Either you go to Mrs Thing in the flat next door . . .'

'No.'

'Why not? I know we hardly ever see her, but she did

offer once in a half-hearted sort of way. If-you-ever-get-stuck sort of thing. I'll go and . . .'

'No.' Geraldine had been in there only once, just after they had moved in. Mum had wanted to meet them, to explain about having to practise her cello. Mrs Taylor had asked questions like 'And what does your husband do?' and said she hoped there wouldn't be noisy parties like musicians had. 'I'm an orchestral player, Mrs Taylor,' her mother had said in a curiously flat voice, 'not a punk rock groupie. And Geraldine and I have lived by ourselves for the past ten years.' Mrs Taylor's eyes had turned hard. 'I suppose you wanted a career, too. You young women . . .' Geraldine had seen the look in her mother's eyes and had not been surprised by Mrs Taylor's voice trailing off into silence. The hallway where they talked smelled musty, sour and old.

'No,' Geraldine repeats.

Her mother snaps off the music lamp and the gas fire, leaving the room as murky as the dusk outside. Geraldine follows her along to the kitchen. 'Or what?'

'Or what . . . What?' says her mother, opening a tin of spaghetti.

'You said either I go to Mrs Thing or . . . Sorry, Mum, I'm sorry really, I can't help it if . . .'

'I know, Jellybean. I know. Of course you can't.' She turns from the stove and Geraldine sees to her relief that her eyes are not angry. Her hands reach out, the signal for a cuddle. 'Of course, you can't, little one.'

She sighs.

From inside the rough cardigan, Geraldine smells the warm perfume her mother always uses. She hears the clunk of the toaster popping up. A hand feels her forehead, then tips her chin up and Geraldine knows from her smile that Mum has thought of something.

'I know. You can come with me tonight. You haven't

been since that first night when the manager shouted you an ice-cream sundae so enormous that you couldn't finish it. Remember? And I broke a string in the middle of the "Waltz of the Flowers".'

'Do I have any choice?'

'Not really. I haven't time to ring around and organize another baby-sitter. I'll shout you an ice-cream sundae this time. It'll help your sore throat. How's that?'

Now it is Geraldine's turn to sigh, but she tries to hide it. Her throat is hurting and she would much rather have spent the evening tucked up in bed listening to Leanne.

'The spaghetti's burning, Mum.'

2

Inside their small car, the cello occupies the front seat, Geraldine the back. That is the way it has always been.

Geraldine suspects that her mother is not what other people would call a good driver. Unsmiling men in white helmets had more than once bent their faces to the window and written on bits of paper, even after a lot of talk and joking. The encounter invariably left her mother sounding off for the rest of the journey about officious people with nothing better to do; yet Geraldine suspects that she does drive faster than she should. Regularly the brakes go on hard, throwing Geraldine against the back of the driver's seat and leaving her feeling rather ill. Tonight, with not much time to spare, it is stop-start all the way.

'Idiot,' her mother mutters. 'Damn lights.' Then, suddenly, as a big van does a U-turn in front of them, skidding on the wet road, 'Hallelujah!' After that she drives slower and the brakes go on with a gentler touch.

Still, it is something of a treat for Geraldine to be going out at night, a change from baby-sitters and the familiar sound of the Mini pulling out of the garage. Geraldine tries to forget her sore throat and is surprised to discover how frequently a person needs to swallow.

'Did you bring something to read, Jellybean?'

'Yes.'

'I'll find you a place near us until nine o'clock. After that you'll have to curl up in the manager's office for an hour. I'm sure he won't mind, if I talk nicely to him. Children are only allowed until nine o'clock.'

'That's stupid.'

'I agree, but I don't make the rules.'

The car is creeping along a narrow side-street: high brick walls, people with umbrellas, many wet cars reflecting the street-lamps above, and rain, always rain.

'Here's one,' says her mother triumphantly, nipping the Mini into a tiny space. She pulls on the handbrake with a flourish. 'We start in five minutes. Come on Jellybean.'

Her mother's black velvet cape, the one she always wears when going out to play, swirls magnificently over the wet footpath as they hurry around the corner. She carries the cello with ease, as though it were a light suitcase.

At the foot of the stairs leading up to the restaurant entrance they pause to shake the rain from their clothes. Geraldine looks at her mother in some awe; those recently tired eyes are now glinting and the face inside the black hood is hardly recognizable as her own mother. Beautiful, in fact.

'Are you nervous?'

'Of course. Always. Always a little.'

The violinist is already tuning up as they come through the archway into the main part of the restaurant, where the air is warm and smoky. Mum sweeps off towards the low stage at the far end. Geraldine hangs back, conscious of the contrast between her mother's grand entrance and herself creeping in, conspicuous in her yellow school raincoat. She can feel curious eyes on her. There are, she notes sourly, no children at any of those tables, or those, or – even less likely – over there, at a bar where people are sitting on tall stools. She wishes she had changed her school shoes for her one pair of going-out shoes. She feels such a . . . such a lump!

To her relief, Geraldine notices a spare table, tucked in behind a pillar and a huge plant with smooth shiny leaves. Before she has even sat down, the music stand is up, the cello is coming out of its case and her mother is talking brightly to the other two players. Then comes the sound of the cello being tuned to the repeated piano note, and the violinist doing the same on a higher note. Geraldine takes off her raincoat and buries her nose in her book. She is sure that people are still looking but soon, after the trio has played four or five pieces, she feels safe enough to look up and watch them listening, talking, eating, drinking – and clapping too, at the end of each piece. The violinist gives a little bow and her mother smiles graciously. The pianist, whom Geraldine can only just see through the gap between the lid and the grand piano, scowls and fusses with her music. The music itself Geraldine doesn't find very interesting: its texture is thin, with no beat, and no big rich sound like the orchestra. Her book is better.

After a while, the table shakes and she looks up to see her mother sitting on the chair opposite.

'We have a break every forty-odd minutes. Union rules. Do you want me to order you an ice-cream sundae?'

'Yes, please.'

'What flavour?'

'Chocolate.'

'Do you want to come and say hello to the others? You'll remember meeting them before.'

'Do I have to?'

'Not if you don't want to.'

'I'd rather sit here.'

Her mother is looking over at the other two musicians who are now talking loudly with a group at one of the front tables. Geraldine has the uncomfortable feeling that her mother is finding her presence tonight something of an embarrassment.

'Jellybean, I have to go. That man sitting there is an agent. If we're nice to him and he likes our music, it could mean more work.'

'What's an agent?'

'He hires people for jobs like this. Television work, art gallery openings, banquets, big weddings, you know.'

'Oh.' No wonder her mother's eyes had been watchful. 'I'm okay, Mum. You go.'

She does so, promptly, to laugh with the agent and his party. A glass of fizzy wine is poured for her in a strange wide glass. Geraldine, her chin resting on her hands, watches closely. This is a mother she has not seen before, a public mum who belongs to someone or something else. Geraldine is not sure she even likes her very much. What's more, the ice-cream sundae does not arrive. Didn't her clever-laughing-everybody's-favourite mother remember it was supposed to help her sore throat? She must have forgotten all about that as well as her daughter.

Geraldine slides further down into her chair. She is beginning to feel very tired as well as bored. Not even the sundae, when it eventually does arrive, chocolate sauce dribbling thickly down the insides of the glass, can do much to help. She is still trying to decide whether to stand up to eat from this ridiculous glass and so appear foolish, or to lift the whole lot down onto her lap, when she hears a voice.

'Do you mind if I join you?'

The man standing behind the chair opposite, his hands resting on the curved back, is bearded, dark-suited, not young. Geraldine cannot see his eyes behind the glasses, but something about the way he is standing, the angle of his head, suggests to her that he is as uncomfortable as she is, even shy. And that, for Geraldine, accustomed to her mother's musician friends, is something new in an adult. When she does not immediately reply, he hesitates.

'Sometimes . . . ah . . . people prefer not to be disturbed. If you would . . .'

'No. I mean . . . Yes. I mean . . . I don't mind.' How

could she? One look around has told her there are no other seats free.

He sits down almost apologetically and looks at her. Geraldine decides she will lift the sundae down onto her lap.

'My name is Gerald. Gerald Matthews.'

That's odd, she thinks, but she will keep her name to herself. He is holding out his hand. Geraldine is puzzled until it occurs to her that he wants to shake her hand. She fumbles in her lap with the saucer on which the glass is sitting, doubting that she can hold everything together with only her left hand. The risk of chocolate all over her skirt seems to be considerable.

'Please, don't worry,' he says hurriedly, withdrawing his hand. 'Of course, you are somewhat occupied.'

'I'm sorry, I . . .'

'Please, think no more.' After a short silence, he adds. 'I saw you come in with your mother.'

She nods.

He continues, 'I couldn't imagine why else you would be here, alone. It wouldn't be for the food and obviously not the company.'

'Why are you here?' She can't bring herself to add. 'Alone'. She always thought that the point of going to restaurants was to go with somebody.

'The music. Light music to be sure, but excellently played. It reminds me of English seaside hotels. Listen.' And they both listen to the rest of the piece which is fast and loud, some kind of a dance. It finishes with three stamping chords which the three women play with a great flourish. They laugh together as the clapping breaks out. Geraldine notices her visitor claps only briefly, but as though he means it.

'Did you know it? Brahms' "Hungarian Dance, Number Five".'

'No.'

'Are you learning an instrument? Please note,' he adds quickly, 'I'm not asking are you going to play the cello like your mother. I expect you must get very bored with that question.'

'I do.' This is not strictly true; nobody asks her at all much, which is almost worse. She scrapes carefully around the inside of the glass for the final streaks of chocolate sauce. 'I learn the piano.'

'Do you enjoy it?'

'Not much.'

'You think you have no feel for the instrument?'

'No.'

'Then why do you learn?'

'My mother thinks it's good for me. She says whatever instrument I want to play, a couple of years at the piano will always stand me in good stead.' That phrase Geraldine can repeat word for word. What she does not add is that there seems to be some sort of barrier to a discussion on the matter ever taking place. Her mother is always too busy, it's too late, too early, she's due at a rehearsal, or late for something else and it's time you went to school, Geraldine.

The music has started up again, slower this time, with her mother playing a solo and the pianist doing lots of rippling things up and down the piano, frowning at her music.

'You wouldn't be able to play like that?'

'No.'

They listen again. Geraldine wishes she had made her sundae last longer, to give her hands something to do.

'I believe your mother plays in the city orchestra as well?'

'Yes.'

'A fine orchestra. She must be very busy with rehearsals, performances, this trio, other sorts of work as well. Very busy.'

'She is.'

'Not an easy life.'

She shrugs. The only mother in all Rooms Nine and Ten . . .

'Not all that much money in it, either.'

True, thinks Geraldine. New clothes *are* a treat.

'Does she teach as well?' he continues.

'No.'

Then he stops looking vague and gives her a brief smile.

'I play the cello, too.'

'Oh.'

'You don't seem very impressed.'

'All my mother's friends play something.'

'And there isn't one of all those instruments you'd like to play?'

Geraldine, taken aback, considers carefully. She has decided she doesn't like this man with all his questions, even if he has said some nice things about her mother and has a nice face and talks to her like a person. She wonders who he is – another agent? But then an agent wouldn't be the slightest bit interested in her, Geraldine, age ten years and four months, wearing a yellow plastic raincoat with skinny wet hair and freckles and teeth so funny that her mother has to spend a thousand dollars when she's thirteen to have them straightened.

What answer would annoy him the most: double-bass? Trombone? Women don't often play those things. The recorder? She knows that has no place in an orchestra. Or will she say she doesn't want to play anything at all, that she hates music. Percussion, perhaps . . .

'The celeste.'

His eyes widen. 'My dear girl, in all orchestral literature there is only one piece for the celeste commonly performed. Tchaikovsky. "Dance of the Sugar Plum Fairy", *Casse Noisette*. A mere trifle. I suppose there's Bartok, but . . .'

'I know.' That exquisite little dance, part of a cassette she occasionally played at home, had always fascinated her.

'Do you know there's a charming story about Tchaikovsky's celeste? He heard it in Paris and wrote it into his ballet score. That opening night in . . . ah, 1892, I think it was . . . at the Maryinsky Theatre in St Petersburg, or what we now call Leningrad, was the first time that anyone in Russia had ever heard one. Imagine it, a completely *new* sound! Tchaikovsky kept the music and the instrument in the greatest secrecy until the opening night because he was afraid another composer like Rimsky-Korsakoff or Glazanov might beat him to it.'

Geraldine knew none of this, and tried not to look interested.

'I fear you would not be able to get much work as a celeste player. You would have to work as a pianist too, which is a very competitive field, and you say you don't like the piano.'

'I didn't say I wanted to be a musician.'

'Ah, that's different.'

'Actually,' says Geraldine, to her astonishment spilling to this stranger a secret she had never before told anyone, ever, 'I'd like to be a conductor.'

'That's different again. May I ask why?'

'If I was the conductor I'd be in charge. I'd be noticed. I'm getting a bit sick of always waiting for Mum to finish playing the Tchaikovsky Fourth or something and all her friends in the orchestra looking straight through me as if I wasn't there at all.' She stops, slightly breathless, appalled at what she has given away.

'Interesting.' His head is nodding slightly. 'Interesting. Do you go to lots of rehearsals?'

'Saturdays. School holidays. Lots.'

'I'm surprised they let you.'

'Why? I just sit there. I've always just sat there.'

'It's not usual. Even well-behaved children.'

'I suppose they're just used to me. I've always gone with Mum to rehearsals, long as I can remember.'

Geraldine knows what he is thinking. Where's her father? Why doesn't she spend some time with him? Well, she isn't going to give him that satisfaction.

'Do you play the cello as well as my mother?'

He hesitates. 'I might have done, once.'

'Why not now?'

Again the hesitation. The music finishes with a dramatic roll on the piano, and more laughter and clapping. Geraldine notices her mother lay her cello on its side. It must be time for another break. Her visitor, peering around the pillar, has obviously noticed this too.

'You must excuse me, Geraldine. I . . . have an appointment shortly.' He is standing. A small nod of his head. 'Please excuse me. I have enjoyed meeting you. Will you tell your mother I enjoyed her music, too.' And he is hurrying away between the tables towards the door and seems to dissolve into the smoky atmosphere.

'Who was that?' says her mother, sitting down on the empty chair opposite. 'He left in a hurry.'

'I don't know.'

'He wasn't worrying you, I hope. You get some funny people . . .'

'No. Oh no. Only . . .' How had he known her name? She was quite sure she hadn't told him.

'Only what?'

'He . . . said he played the cello, too.'

'Probably in pit orchestras twenty years ago. His back-view looked a bit moth-eaten to me.'

Unkind, thinks Geraldine. 'You don't know that. He might be very good. He might be . . .'

'A central European emigre who once played with the Berlin Philharmonic,' says her mother lightly. But there is a troubled expression on her face Geraldine doesn't understand, as if she is trying to remember something. She is still looking towards the doorway through which he left. 'Did he have an accent?'

'No. I don't think so. Perhaps sort of English.' After a pause, she adds, 'His name was Gerald something.'

Her mother looks at her sharply.

'Gerald? What was the something?'

'I can't remember. He told me to tell you he enjoyed your music.'

After a long pause, her mother stands abruptly. 'It's nine o'clock, Jellybean. The barman is giving me dirty looks.'

Geraldine allows herself to be led from the huge room, along the cool passageway and into a small office with 'Manager' on the door.

'I've told the manager you're here. He might pop in from time to time. How do you feel?'

'My throat's sore.'

'I'll give you an aspirin when we get home. Curl up in that chair. I finish at ten. That's not long.' The door is closing. 'You've got your book. It won't seem too long.'

She is wrong, thinks Geraldine as her book goes stale on her. It seems a very long time indeed. Now she knows how a doll feels when it is put away in a cupboard, listening to other people enjoying themselves. Or how Cinderella felt left behind, or worse, how Cinderella felt walking into the ballroom with no one taking any notice of her. There are no fairy godmothers here, she thinks, looking at the charts and lists and advertising posters on the walls. The manager doesn't even bother or is too busy to 'pop in'.

Geraldine has begun to hate the sound of the music coming through the closed door.

3

All too soon after she has climbed into bed and pulled the duvet over her ears, Geraldine is being shaken awake again.

'Jellybean, time to get up.'

Then, more urgently, 'Jellybean, you've got to get moving. I've left you as long as I possibly could.'

She opens one eye to a room brilliant with winter sunshine and rivers of water running down the insides of the window panes. That means it is cold, very cold, outside her bed.

She groans in protest.

'Quarter-past eight,' the voice goes on. 'I have to be at rehearsal at nine. You must get *up*, Jellybean.'

Rehearsals, always rehearsals. She almost wishes it were a weekday and she was going to school. But no, it is Saturday and her mother is doing the Tchaikovsky Fourth. And her throat is still sore.

In the sunless kitchen, the porridge pot is sending a shaft of steam half-way to the ceiling. Her pottery bowl sits waiting on the bare table.

'Don't feel like porridge, Mum.'

'No porridge? But I made it for you specially.'

'Sorry.'

'Never mind. The cat'll eat it. What do you want then?'

'Nothing. Toast. I'm not hungry.'

'Is your throat still sore?'

Ah, she remembers; in the day-time, at home, Mum remembers.

'Yes.'

'More?'

She tests. 'About the same.'

Two mugs of fresh coffee arrive on the table.

'Well, drink some of this. How do you feel otherwise?'

'Tired.'

'And a bit disgruntled, eh? Last night wasn't a great success, I know. It's not like that every night at closing time, Jellybean,' she says, making excuses.

Geraldine, after being woken from her curled-up sleep in the manager's office, remembers only stumbling down the stairs after the cello case, the sounds of men shouting, a man's figure falling to the ground, others standing over it, arguing. A brawl, her mother said, as they hurried away towards the car. And then there was the siren of a police car sounding clear over the car engine noise. She could see its blue flashing light through the rain as they drove away, and worse, the siren of an ambulance behind them.

'I didn't like that,' she says, her hands cupped around the warmth of the coffee mug.

'Neither did I,' said her mother. 'I'm just sorry it had to be the one night you came. I sometimes see the occasional drunk weaving off down the road, not usually anything like that.'

They drink in silence.

'Time to go,' says her mother crisply. 'Better bring your parka this morning. It'll be cold in the hall.'

And so it is, like walking into a fridge. They are early; only the harpist is already in her seat, dropping icicles of sound into the silence. At the back of the stage two percussion men are setting up drums, cymbals, gong, timpani.

Quickly now, the musicians arrive. They unpack their instruments and greet each other as though it was one whole month and not one day since they had last seen each other. They laugh, and take the gloves from their hands and rub them to keep warm. Geraldine has noticed that musicians take very great care of their hands.

She chooses a seat at the back, near one of the electric heaters which has just been turned on. There are two or three other people sitting about who are obviously not players, one a boy not much older than herself. A few of the players, her mother's special friends, greet her. Many do not, so that she wonders – not for the first time – if she is invisible to them.

Now there is a whole row of black soldiers standing open along the side of the hall. Some, especially those belonging to the double-basses, are even bigger and blacker than her mother's. Over the seats lie all sorts of empty cases: slender ones for the violins and flutes, fat ones for the French horns, long ones for the trombones and bassoons, neat rectangles for the smaller woodwind. Geraldine knows exactly what will come out of each case.

The oboe note sounds clearly through the conversation, and each section of the orchestra tunes up. First the strings, then all the woodwind, all the brass and finally all together. The players and their instruments fall silent. From the second row of the cellos, her mother sends her a small smile. Geraldine knows that the thin bald man who has been sitting in the front row reading some music will now stand and walk to the rostrum. He has a small white stick in his hand.

'Good morning, ladies and gentlemen.' Some conductors chat for a bit, or crack a few jokes, or talk about the music they are to rehearse. Not this one. He says nothing more before slowly lifting his baton. After a long, very long pause, the music begins.

For Geraldine, it is a miracle: from the hollow drone of an orchestra tuning up to the magic of the trumpets proclaiming the opening of the Tchaikovsky Fourth. Now she knows why she is still feeling vaguely unhappy about her conversation with that strange cellist last night. She isn't dragged to rehearsals. She doesn't want to be a conductor simply so that people will notice her. It isn't that at all. She is happy to come because the orchestra is her mother's life and therefore hers too, and she just can't imagine a life without music, this music, the music of a fine orchestra.

The music makes her think of the great oak trees in the park near home, of standing on the headland at Muriwai and watching the surf roll in from the ocean. It can start a tingle which grabs her behind the ears and travels down her spine and makes her feel so full of sound she could burst. It can bring tears to her eyes, or make her want to dance with joy. It also makes her forget that no one ever asks her home from school to play, that she has never had a midnight feast, and that she has never seen her father, not even a photograph.

Geraldine's fingers are imitating the plucking movements of the string players as they start off on the third movement, all pizzicato, when she feels the seat shake a little as someone sits down at the other end of the row near the main door. The pizzicato movement finishes with a little chuckle. The string players relax their fingers and pick up their bows. Geraldine, glancing casually along the row of seats, is so surprised by what she sees that when the orchestra suddenly crashes into the next movement absolutely fortissimo, with cymbals, timpani, everything, she nearly falls out of her seat.

There is no doubt about it. There is the same beard, the big slightly curved nose, the rather sad-looking clothes – and the same intent air of listening to the music. And when he finally turns at the very end of the symphony – though Geraldine has the feeling all along that he knows she is there – there is the same smile, oddly shy for an adult.

She knows better than to move before the conductor has said whatever he wants to say. When she sees the players begin to talk and stand up, she moves up the row and sits down next but one to her friend from last night. She leans over the arm of the seat.

'Why did you leave so quickly last night?'

'Good morning, Geraldine. I thought I'd see you again today.'

'You didn't want to meet my mother.'

'Not then, no.'

'Why not? Everyone likes my mother.'

In the brief silence, she notices that his hands, in thick gloves, are restless.

'It didn't . . . seem appropriate.'

Geraldine, perplexed, looks over at her mother, now talking with the woman who shares her music stand. She is smiling, clearly sharing a joke or a good story.

'That was a good run-through,' he says. 'It should be a fine concert tonight.'

'Are you going?'

'Of course.'

'I've never seen you at a rehearsal before . . . have I?' That might explain her mother's frown last night in the restaurant. There were always a few odd people sitting around during rehearsals.

'No, I've only just moved to the city.'

'Where did you live before that?'

The Maori name he speaks with care is unfamiliar to her.

'Where's that?'

'North. Up north, as you say. North of Whangarei.'

'Why did you live there?'

Now, almost for the first time, he turns to look at her. The absurd thought flashes through her mind that this strange, shy man might be her father. Surely he wouldn't be as old as this, as tired-looking. But his very next words settle the matter.

'My wife . . . was a New Zealander. When we came

out from the UK it became clear that she needed a better climate than Auckland. The humidity, the damp didn't suit her. We were advised by her doctors to move north.'

'Was she sick?'

His hands become still and his face turns again toward the orchestra.

'She died seven months ago.'

'I'm . . . I'm sorry,' says Geraldine. It is the first time anyone has told her of a death.

'She made me promise, not long before she died, that I would come back to the city and start playing again. Living in the north, a village life, meant that I couldn't follow the only profession for which I was trained.'

'You said you were a cellist.'

'Did I? A cellist, I said. I was, once. Perhaps I still am. Today will tell me whether there's anything left.'

'Why today?'

Those gloved hands are doing a little dance again on his knees.

'After the rehearsal, I'm having an audition with the conductor, and possibly the cello principals. I don't know what their custom is in this orchestra.'

'You're nervous, aren't you?' His eyes have the same glint as she had noticed in her mother's last night.

'Yes. Very. I thought if I came and listened to the rehearsal it might calm me down. It seems to have been a mistake. I haven't been so nervous since I was a student in London.'

'You're English?'

'Yes.'

'Did you play in an orchestra in England?'

'A special kind of orchestra.'

'What kind?'

'A theatre orchestra.'

'Oh, not a proper one.' What had her mother said in such scathing tones? A pit orchestra . . .

'What do you mean by that?'

Possibly she has offended him. She hasn't meant to.

'Well, you didn't give concerts, I mean. Like tonight, in the Town Hall.'

He is smiling. 'We gave a concert nearly every night of the week, eleven months of the year. Matinees as well. The Orchestra of the Royal Opera House, Covent Garden. We played with great singers, the best conductors, the greatest dancers, the best in the world.'

'What's an opera house like?'

'You don't know? I suppose not. There's nothing in this country remotely worthy of the name and never likely to be. You have to go to Sydney for that.'

His eyes are closed.

'Imagine a very big theatre, with tier upon tier of seats, a crystal chandelier in the high dome of its roof. A vast stage framed in gold, curtained in scarlet. Staircases of marble, walls of mirrors in carved frames, fine paintings. The music of Wagner, Verdi, Puccini, Richard Strauss, Bellini, Tchaikovsky, Stravinsky. In the gallery, students who have stood for hours in the snow to get tickets. In the stalls and boxes, people of wealth and culture. Some are there simply because it's the done thing, but their patronage is valuable, notwithstanding. And in the pit, a full symphony orchestra in evening dress: seventy, eighty, sometimes a hundred musicians, expectant, waiting for the conductor to appear and that wonderful curtain to be swept aside.'

Geraldine whispers, 'That is where you played?'

'I did. For seven years, full-time.'

Geraldine breaks the silence between them.

'Why did you come out here then?'

'My wife's illness had just been confirmed. I couldn't

have continued at the Garden because of the night work, the odd hours. She wanted to come home. She could be nursed in the sun and I could join this orchestra. That was the theory, but it just didn't work out that way. I hardly touched my cello in four years. Somehow I just couldn't.'

Knowing that nothing she could say would sound right to break another long silence, Geraldine watches the orchestra move back to their seats. For a moment she has a very odd thought that Gerald is not talking to her at all, but rather to her mother who is now staring up at them both from her seat among the cellos. Even as the oboe note gives its mournful call and she begins the tuning-up ritual along with the other string players, her mother's gaze does not alter. It is as though she can hardly believe what she sees. Yet Geraldine knows she is not looking at her, but rather at the bearded man beside her.

'So,' he continues, in a whisper now, as the orchestra waits for the piano soloist to adjust her stool for the concerto. 'So, I've been practising a lot, several hours a day. Apart from selling the house, moving to Auckland, I've done little else. It has helped to keep busy.'

Geraldine has seen the conscious effort needed for her mother to turn her attention to the music in front of her. The pianist is still adjusting her seat and wiping the keyboard with a handkerchief.

Gerald has not quite finished. 'I've told you my dream, Geraldine. Most of it is over now but I have one hope left. You tell me about yours. A conductor, you said? Is that really your dream?'

4

Gerald's question goes unanswered as the piano concerto begins. Instead, Geraldine studies the conductor. She notices how carefully he is watching the pianist. Between the movements there is complete silence, so that she dare not attempt even a whispered reply. She is not too sure what she is going to say, anyway.

After the final dramatic finish, they sit in silence for a few minutes. The orchestra players talk and shuffle around and get out new music. Her mother seems engrossed in talking to the player next door again and does not look up at them at all. Geraldine is grateful that her new friend is not pressing her for an answer. Finally she says, 'Have you ever . . .? Conducted an orchestra, I mean.'

'No. I never felt inclined to try, even as a student.'

'How do people start?'

'The love of music is the first thing. Do you think you love music enough?'

Enough? How much is enough? she wonders.

'Enough,' he answers as if she has spoken, 'to study several instruments, learn to read scores, theory, harmony, counterpoint, work your way up through student orchestras, chamber groups, professional orchestras, study the world's great literature, philosophy, art, architecture, learn the techniques of rehearsing, accompanying . . .'

His list hangs unfinished in the silence as again the conductor raises his baton and the players, a little tired now, lift their instruments. The opening of the next piece is very quiet and gentle. The conductor almost seems to be shaping the music out of the air with his hands. Geraldine feels overwhelmed at the thought of everything she would have to achieve before she could even attempt to conduct an orchestra. She hadn't realized how much was involved.

After only a few bars of the new piece she becomes aware that Gerald has sat forward and is gripping the back of the seat in front of him. She is reminded of a bird about to fly away. After only a few bars more, he is gone, disappearing through the swing doors at the back of the hall. Geraldine watches him go, startled by the abruptness of his departure. As soon as the music is loud enough for her to dare, she moves into the empty seat at the end of the row and then tip-toes up the aisle towards the doors, praying that her mother is too intent on her music to notice. She has never stirred out of her seat at a rehearsal before.

The foyer is empty, with the wind blowing in through the open door from the street; the pavement outside is also empty and cold. Geraldine looks up and down the footpath and across the broad street to the shops on the other side. Most of them are open but have few customers. The Indian fruit shop next door to the hall is empty, too. Behind her, the orchestra's music can be clearly heard.

Then she sees him, leaning against a bare tree further along the road. As she runs towards him, the music fades.

'That is the second time you've . . . .' she begins but even from ten metres away, something in his expression forbids her to say more.

'I wish someone had told me they were doing that piece.'

'The one they're playing now?'

'There was an overture scheduled, not that.'

Geraldine thinks. 'I heard something about some parts not arriving in time, from Australia or somewhere.'

He nods, an I-might-have-known sort of nod. During the long silence she notices that he has lit a cigarette. He begins to walk round and round the tree.

'I didn't know grown-ups got so nervous,' says Geraldine in what she hopes is a sympathetic voice.

'Nervous? That's only part of it.'

'What's the other part?'

He stops his walking, abruptly, as though he has come to a decision. 'I'm not playing this morning. I can't.'

'Why not? You've been practising for months, you said.'

Then he looks at her and Geraldine sees the tears behind his glasses.

'I haven't heard that music since my wife died. It was written by Wagner as a birthday present for his wife. An orchestra stole into their house at dawn and that is how she was woken.'

'That's beautiful,' says Geraldine, remembering those tender opening bars.

'We used to play it, too, on our birthdays. Hers would have been in two weeks' time.'

For the second time this morning, Geraldine can think of absolutely nothing to say.

'So you see I can't go and play. Not now.'

'Why not?'

'I haven't prepared enough. My technique, it's gone, rusty. I've been deluding myself to think I could ever . . .'

'You promised.'

It is strange that she feels she knows him well enough to be so blunt.

'Promised what?' he says, looking at her suspiciously.

'You said you'd promised your . . . your wife you'd start playing again.'

'I did but . . . Well, I can join an amateur chamber group, play string quartets, teach, play for the local Gilbert and Sullivan . . .'

'Is that what she meant?'

Silence.

'Didn't you say you'd been practising hard, all the time for months and months?'

'I did say that.'

'My mother says it's like riding a bicycle.'

He almost laughs. Behind him, she notices a group of people leave the hall, instrument cases in their hands. Three or four violins, a French horn, one trombone.

'They've finished. Mum will be wondering where I am. Come on, they'll be waiting for you too.'

He hesitates only briefly, smiles, and stubs out his cigarette on the knobbled tree trunk. They have reached the entrance before Geraldine realizes that she is leading him by the hand.

5

As they drive home along the empty weekend streets, Geraldine strokes the back of her mother's neck and asks, 'Have you ever been to an opera house, Mum? The Royal Opera House, Covent Garden?'

'Those two years I was studying in London, yes, lots of times. Why?'

'What's it like?'

'Covent Garden? Fantastic place, all red and gold inside. Little lampshades everywhere, bit like a French cafe, someone once said. But atmosphere, glamour – plenty of it. We had student tickets up in the gods, for every ballet and opera. The orchestra's good.'

So he must be good, good enough for Mum's orchestra.

'Why do you ask?'

'Oh nothing. That man . . . the one . . .'

'The same man you met last night, wasn't it? Gerald something. The cellist?'

'Yes.'

'You seemed to be having quite a chat.' In the rear vision mirror Geraldine can see her mother is looking at her and not at the road.

'He played at Covent Garden. For seven years, he said.'

When there is no reaction, except her mother's eyebrows rising slightly and another sharp look in the mirror, Geraldine says, 'Will he get in the orchestra? He's doing an audition now.'

'I know. Maybe he will.' Her mother jams on the brakes as a traffic light turns orange. 'Damn.'

Somehow dissatisfied with her mother's apparent lack

of interest, Geraldine sits back and watches a muddy laughing group of hockey players about her own age cross the road at the lights. She has decided not to tell her mother anything more about her new friend. When they had returned to the rehearsal, Gerald had gone straight to unpack his cello standing by itself at the back. She had not said goodbye or even good luck; that, she knew, was the way he wanted it. If her mother had noticed her absence, she had not mentioned it. Unusually, she had packed up her cello and music with a minimum of chat to her friends and said it was quicker out a side door, this way Geraldine.

As the car moves off from the lights, Geraldine asks, 'Don't you go to the auditions, Mum?'

'No, just the Maestro and two principals.'

'What do you have to do?'

'Play something demanding, like one of the Bach unaccompanied suites. And you have to do some sight-reading, something really testing.'

'Would you get nervous?'

'Of course. I'd be weak at the knees, especially for the sight-reading, which is always difficult.' They wait at another set of traffic lights and see yet another group of laughing girls, netball players this time with tiny skirts above their pink thighs. Their breath is misty in the crisp air.

'I wish you played some sport, Jellybean, joined a team or something.'

'I hate teams.'

'So you say.' After a pause, she adds casually, 'What else did your friend, Gerald . . . What else did he tell you?'

'Nothing much.' The eyes in the mirror are beginning to disconcert her. Geraldine looks deliberately out the window. It's not, she feels, the answer her mother wanted, but it's the answer she's going to get.

'Let's go to the park, Mum,' she says suddenly.

Her mother yawns loudly. 'I'm tired, Jellybean.'

'Please. It's a lovely day.'

They drive another block. 'Okay. We'll get a hamburger and take it to the playground.' Her voice sounds more enthusiastic now. 'Blow away a few cobwebs.'

Geraldine puts her arms over the back of the seat and gives her mother a big squeeze.

'Careful, you'll throttle me, Jellybean.'

The hamburger shop in the next block is small, a bit shabby, but it makes the best hamburgers in town. They order two super-size hamburgers, one pineapple fritter, and two cans of juice. Her mother, as usual, gets into conversation with the hamburger man, but Geraldine takes no interest. She cannot put Gerald out of her mind. He is playing now, at this moment, something demanding. Whatever will he do if he makes a mess of it? Will he forget all about the orchestra, all about her? She might never know.

'You're quiet today, Jellybean,' her mother says as they walk away from the parked car towards the playground, looking for a sheltered place to have their picnic. 'Over there, that'll do, under that tree. I hope you're not sickening for something, with that sore throat. Perhaps we shouldn't . . .'

'No, I'm all right. Really,' says Geraldine hurriedly. Her throat is still sore, but only when she swallows, and she knows that the afternoon is hers alone. No other cellists, no agents: just her Mum, Ms Anna-liese Waite, who will scramble up the cargo net, slide down the fireman's pole, try the slide, the flying fox and the maypole, pull up her jeans and splash in the wintry water of the paddling pool, and help catch the boatmen swimming in it. Together they will ignore the other children, the bullies who push to the front of the queues, the toddlers being helped by their dads. They will also ignore the curious looks of other people's children at the sight of an adult whooping down a slide or launching herself off the flying fox. The afternoon is Geraldine's and it would need more than a sore throat to take it away from her.

After a satisfyingly long time, her mother's hair has grown untidy and her cheeks flushed. She looks at her watch. 'If we're going to walk up the hill, we'd better go now, Jellybean. I'd like to have a short rest when we get home, and wash my hair. It's the Tchaikovsky tonight.'

The concert. Always another concert. Geraldine has forgotten, but not her mother, who never forgets about her music, the next recital, the next concert. She realizes a little guiltily that she has also forgotten about Gerald and his audition, which would surely be finished by now. She imagines him packing up his cello, leaving the big empty hall, alone.

'Mum,' she says as they set off across a wide field, 'how do people *become* conductors?'

'What?'

'How do people start? Not the famous ones who fly around the world and make lots of records – the ordinary ones, I mean, like Maestro who lives here and does operas and school concerts and stuff like that.'

'An ordinary conductor?' says her mother thoughtfully. 'That's a contradiction in terms. Musicians are never ordinary, least of all conductors.'

'Well how do they start?'

'They all play at least one instrument very well. Usually piano, or violin as concert-master, though not always. I don't know – just sort of graduate from playing in the orchestra to conducting it. Takes a long time. Years and years and years. It's not a young man's job.'

'Have you, ever?'

'As a student, to records, the student orchestra once or

twice. I hated it. I have to make my music myself, with my own fingers, not at arm's length.'

'Do women?'

'Not often. Oh, you get lots of women conducting school choirs, youth orchestras, the grass roots things, but not big professional orchestras. There's a few in America, one who conducts opera – she's one of the best.'

So it can be done. 'In a big opera house?'

Her mother nods. They are both panting now. Above them the obelisk on the summit shines silver.

'Getting tired, Jellybean?'

'No.' Not true, but these outings are precious.

'Do you want to go to the top? You feel okay?'

'Yes.'

They walk in silence as the road becomes steeper and the wind stronger against their cheeks. Several cars pass them. They frighten away a few sheep, thick with winter wool and bulging with lambs.

'Not long for those old girls,' says her mother. 'Lambs in August – I can never understand why lambs come in the wettest, coldest month.'

Geraldine longs to pat the springy woollen backs, but she knows that the sheep will, despite their bulk, run away from her and leap faster down the steep grass than she would ever dare.

'Nearly there.'

Very soon they are standing breathless on the summit, silent before the immensity of the city below and the cold blue of the two harbours, north and south.

'Our house is . . . down there?' says Geraldine, pointing to the flat tree-lined streets leading away from the foot of the hill.

'Right. There's your school, see? And the hills,' she points, 'where we stayed with friends last summer. Remember? Not far from the television transmitter. And behind there, the beach.' Their favourite west coast beach; surf, spray and baking black sand stretching north as far as the eye could see.

This is Geraldine's world, and her city – houses, streets, cars, trees and hills like the one they are standing on; harbours, wharves, ships, the harbour bridge. How little she knows of it all. How tiny her world is, between home and school, piano lessons, the rehearsal hall, the park and the dairy up the road. Summer holidays they spend at some beach or other with her mother's friends, but the other children think she's peculiar because she doesn't want to play their games or go for long tramps in the bush.

One day she will escape. Circling the base of the obelisk and the single grave behind the railings, Geraldine smiles to herself. They'll see.

6

They get up late on Sunday morning. Geraldine is relieved to find her throat is hardly sore at all. Although rare, visits to the doctor have to be fitted into her mother's busy schedule and always leave her feeling guilty. Friends visit before lunch to drink wine and stay to eat French bread and salami. The concert, she hears, went well. It is nearly dark when they begin to leave.

And the audition? She hears nothing mentioned, nothing of a cellist called Gerald. She asks for the television to be put in her bedroom so that she can watch a film. She does her homework, finishes a book, plays with the cat in the backyard and goes to the dairy to get a Sunday paper for her mother and an ice-cream as the pay-off, but all the time she cannot stop wondering about him. That hand holding the cigarette had been trembling.

How will she find out? The casual question, she decides, will be best.

'Mum . . .' she says walking into the kitchen after the last friend has gone. 'Did you . . .?'

But her mother is already talking.

'Jellybean, tell me. What do you think of the idea of a kid conducting the orchestra at a youth concert? Something straightforward, of course.'

'What age?'

'Oh, your age. No, probably a bit older. Early teens.'

Her heart gives a great leap, but she says casually, 'Oh, okay, I suppose.'

'Okay? That's all?'

A vision flies before her eyes. Herself in a black dress,

walking onto the platform through the little aisle between first and second violins, stepping up onto the rostrum. The audience clapping, even before she starts. A small bow. She turns, raises the baton. All the players lift their instruments, they look at her . . .

'You don't mean,' she says, 'just those school concerts where you poke a little kid up in front and play that silly bit of music with the toy whistles and things.' Most years since Geraldine was a J One, the orchestra has come to her school and done just that. The kid loved it, of course, and the rest of the school, but Geraldine who knew about real music found it embarrassing.

'That silly bit of music, as you say, is Haydn's "Toy Symphony". It's a very famous piece.'

'It's *silly*. All those cuckoos and rattles and things. And the grown-ups pretending it's all great fun, even though you're actually all bored to tears . . .'

'Jellybean, you sound positively stuffy. I'm never bored . . .'

'Come on, Mum . . . It *is* silly!'

Her mother looks over from the rack of coffee mugs she is drying and grins. 'Yes, I agree,' she whispers, looking about her with exaggerated concern as though the kitchen was bugged. 'Put these away in the cupboard, will you, Jellybean.'

Geraldine waits for her mother to continue the conversation, but instead she yawns noisily. 'Anything good on telly, Jellybean? Think I might go to bed.'

'It's not even seven o'clock.'

'So what, if you're tired? To be tucked up in bed with a good book is bliss.' She disappears into the bathroom to run a bath.

Geraldine is left putting the coffee mugs away, angry with herself for not saying what she meant. Now the opportunity to tell her mother has gone, and they'll get some other kid to conduct, some cute boy who doesn't know a crochet from a semi-quaver; or worse, some four-eye genius who has done Grade 8 Piano before she has turned eleven.

Another thing Geraldine can't understand: why can't she bring herself to ask directly about the audition? She knows how important it is to Gerald. Music was his whole life, a life he had to give up and now wants so much to get back. She tries to imagine what it would mean to her mother not to be able to play her cello. She'd just fade away. Without her music and the orchestra, she'd be nothing, just another mother living by herself and working in a supermarket or something. One thing is for sure, her mother, Ms Anna-liese Waite, knows more about Mr Gerald Thing, the cellist, than she is letting on.

Geraldine kicks the cupboard door shut.

'Check that the back door chain is up, will you?' comes a voice from the bathroom. It is. There is now nothing left to do but go and play the piano, which Geraldine does, thumpingly.

Coming home from school a few days later, Geraldine finds a note on the kitchen table.

'Jellybean – gone out (2.30) to see a friend in need. Make yourself some afternoon tea. Should be home about 4.30, no later. Mum XXXXXX.'

It was obviously written in a hurry, as Geraldine can only just read the handwriting. The kitchen is cold, and tidier than usual. She turns on the radio and gets a blast of opera, with orchestra and female voice at full stretch. She opens her mouth and mimes, just as she knows pop singers do when they make television programmes, although she's not sure about opera singers. Her arms fling themselves out, in big wide gestures, and she is singing to some point high up in the theatre.

Then her arms become those of a conductor. That's easy,

four-four time. The music becomes very tinkly, like little bells, or it might even be a celeste playing in there. The singer is imitating a bell, too. She holds the orchestra while the last note rings out, high and very distant as though from the top of a mountain, hardly a human voice at all. It is finished. She puts down the bread knife and turns to acknowledge the applause.

'The soprano Joan Sutherland sang the "Bell Song" from *Lakme*,' says the announcer, 'with the Monte Carlo Opera Orchestra conducted by Richard Bonynge.'

'Never heard of him, but an opera house orchestra . . .' Geraldine flips the switch thoughtfully. It is while she is peanut-buttering a piece of bread that she gets an idea. She can practise conducting to one of Mum's tapes, just as Mum said she had to do as a student. The right arm beats the pulse, the left makes the music louder or softer and gives the players their cues. She's worked out that much.

Cramming her peanut-butter sandwich into her mouth, she goes along to the studio which is even colder and tidier than the kitchen. Mum must have had one of her housework binges, a not-very-frequent happening. Choosing the music is not difficult. One of the first tapes her eyes light upon is *Casse Noisette* by Tchaikovsky – the ballet music with the celeste in it.

She moves the music stand into the centre of the room. For a rostrum she needs something low and flat. A chair will be too high and too easy to topple off. A couple of big books? No, they won't be big enough for her feet and besides, she knows her mother is very particular about books. One of the piles of music? Same problem. She looks around the studio, then goes along to her bedroom. Of course, one of the drawers from her dressing table. Perfect. She pulls out the bottom one with only winter jumpers in it, tips the contents on the bed and carries it awkwardly along to the studio.

If she gets on her rostrum, the music stand is too low. She twists one of the screws. The legs collapse. Having fixed those, she tries another screw. The back part, which supports the music, sags and jams her fingers. That sorted out, she tries a third screw. This time the central pole goes clunk to the ground and the whole device looks in danger of falling apart completely. She is beginning to get desperate when she realizes that the only screw left to turn is probably the one which will hold the stand at the height she wants. This turns out to be correct.

For a baton she needs something long and slender, like a knitting needle. This is easily found, in her mother's knitting box in the bedroom. Geraldine finds herself creeping around the room, expecting a voice from under the bed or a figure in the doorway demanding an explanation.

Now, at last, she pushes the play button on the tape deck, and bows to the audience from her rostrum. Turning to the stand, she realizes she has no music on it. One of her mother's cello pieces, all black notes, will do. She resets the tape.

Back on the rostrum, she bows again, and waits poised for the music to start. She closes her eyes, swaying and rocking gently as her arms beat in the way she has seen untold times. She turns the page, with her left hand of course. She needs more volume, so she nips down from the rostrum and turns up the sound. Now the music surrounds her, lifts her away.

Luckily, the music does not carry her so far that she fails to hear the sound of the Mini turning into the drive. Geraldine leaps to the tape deck, pushes the rewind button and knocks over the music stand. The music, five or six pages of it, flies all over the room. She rushes the empty drawer back to her bedroom knocking it against the door frames, and shoves it back into the dressing table, stuffing the clothes in at the same time. Back she goes to the studio to pick up the music and put the music stand away. The baton is easily hidden. She has just tidied the music, but not readjusted the music stand when she hears the back door being shut and the kettle filled for tea. Her heart racing, she lies down on the divan and opens the *Listener*.

'Jellybean? I'm home.'

She is too flustered to answer immediately.

'Where are you, Jellybean?'

'Here.'

Footsteps come up the hall. The studio looks normal, except for the music stand which is still in the middle of the room looking ridiculous – even to Geraldine's eyes – far higher than any cellist would ever use. High enough for a seven foot flautist.

'Hello, Jellybean. Everything okay? Sorry I was late home.' She sits on the edge of the divan and gives Geraldine a kiss. 'My friend was in a bad way. She'd just walked out on her husband and needed a shoulder to weep on. I think I left her better than when I found her.'

Her eyes rest briefly on the music stand. 'Funny, I don't remember leaving that there. Must have been my tidy-up.'

She gets up and absent-mindedly readjusts the height of the stand and puts it back in its normal place. Geraldine holds her breath.

'School okay?'

'Okay.'

It had been a narrow escape. Geraldine had expected to be grilled about why the stand had been fiddled with. She knows her mother hates to find her music things moved or touched. She remembers the thrill of closing her eyes and imagining a great orchestra at her feet.

'I don't mind you being late, Mum.' Any time, Mum. 'Truly.'

7

During the next few weeks, Geraldine comes home from school each day hoping to find another note on the kitchen table and her mother out for an hour. Except for two occasions she is always there, practising or drinking coffee in the kitchen with one or several of her many friends. Geraldine takes the transistor radio and tries to do her conducting in her bedroom, but there isn't much orchestral music on at that time of the day. Even when there is, she dare not turn up the volume.

In desperation, one day when she knows from the schedule pinned above the telephone that her mother will be out all day (rehearsal 9 a.m., television call 1 to 4.00 p.m.), Geraldine walks around the block and returns home instead of going to school. Checking first that the Mini is gone, she quietly creeps up the grass verge of the drive and lets herself in at the back door. A whole day of music stretches in front of her. First, *Casse Noisette*. She rejects the Tchaikovsky Fourth because it reminds her too much of Gerald. He has become a small hole in her life. Her mother has said nothing about him or the youth concert. She tries the *Firebird* – ballet music, much harder with no definite beat she can follow, although she loves the strangeness of the music. Then she conducts the "Carnival of the Animals", using the notes on the cassette which give all the poems and tell what animal each piece is about.

It would have to be Mrs Taylor from the other flat who nearly gives her away. One of the rare rainy Saturdays when there is no rehearsal, Geraldine hears from her bed an early knock at the front door and a murmured conversation. It goes on too long to be the boy collecting paper money or delivering bags for old clothes, or any of the other things that happen on Saturday mornings. Yet her mother doesn't ask the person in.

Eventually the door closes and her mother comes slowly into the bedroom. From the expression on her face, Geraldine knows that somehow she is involved.

'That was Mrs Taylor from next door.'

'Oh?'

'She wanted to let me know that three afternoons recently she has heard very loud music coming from here. So loud it is upsetting her rest.'

'She rests all afternoon?'

'Until four, every day, she says. Well, she's not very well, Geraldine, or very young – you only need to look at her to see that. And she has that grumpy husband to look after. Some days she says she has been woken by loud music.'

Geraldine thinks it best to say nothing.

'Well, I haven't been practising or playing loud symphonies at that time of day,' continues her mother, 'or even had the radio on.'

Geraldine still says nothing.

'Mrs Thing says it only seems to be on afternoons when I'm out and you're at home here by yourself.'

'How does she know that?'

'I suppose she hears the car come in. She says the music on those three occasions started shortly after three and finished about half an hour later, except for one day when . . .'

'I put the radio on sometimes.'

She cannot meet her mother's eyes.

'She says one day she just happened to pass the front window on her way to the letter box. She thought she saw someone dancing around inside the living-room. She couldn't understand why you weren't at school.'

'Mrs Taylor is an old bag,' says Geraldine evenly. 'How dare she peer in our windows. I think that's mean. And I hope you told her so.'

'Not exactly.' Geraldine sees the glimmer of a smile on her face. 'Although basically I agree with you.'

'If we lived in a proper house and not an old one divided into flats,' continues Geraldine, working herself up slightly, 'we'd be able to do what we like. I don't like listening to their telly going every night, or Mr Thing coughing every morning, or the clanks and water every time they go to the loo.'

Her mother laughs briefly. 'Jellybean, you're a trick. I'd love to have a house or townhouse or something to ourselves. As always, it's a . . .'

'. . . question of money,' finishes Geraldine for her, who has heard it all before.

'You remember how awful it was trying to find this flat. The last one was infinitely worse. The Taylors . . . Well, they could be worse neighbours. They're pretty good about my practice.'

Geraldine turns the page of her book.

'Have you been playing the radio very loudly? Or the tape recorder? And have you ever wagged school?'

'The tape deck,' mumbles Geraldine. 'Not very loud really,' she adds untruthfully. Once she'd really given it the works: that final section of the *Firebird*, the dance of the monsters and the Russian hymn at the end. It had set off the tingle in her spine and shot her into space.

'Wagging school?'

There is a short silence.

'One day we got out early, at lunch-time,' she says, feeling dreadful.

'You should have told me.'

'I forgot.' Worse and worse.

'I used to dance, too,' her mother is saying quietly, 'when

I was about ten and going to be a famous ballerina. All round the living-room, and in the back garden when no one was looking.'

Geraldine is about to say that it wasn't *dancing* she'd been doing when she realizes the less she says at this point the better.

'Would you like to learn ballet?'

'No.'

'You just dance because the music makes you? Well, I can understand that. It's a very natural response. We should all do more of it. We lose the ability to express ourselves with our bodies as we grow up.'

Pack it in, Mum. She yawns. 'I still think Mrs Taylor is an old bag. It's none of her business what I do.'

'Only if the noise really is above a reasonable level. I don't mind you using the radio or the tape, Jellybean – you know that – but please remember there's only a wooden wall between us and them.'

Geraldine doesn't reply. At least silly old Mrs Thing had jumped to the wrong conclusion. She wouldn't know a conductor if she fell over one in the street.

'Oh, by the way,' her mother is saying, stopping in the doorway, 'I got my final orchestra schedule for the year. That youth concert I mentioned . . .'

'What about it?'

'Mid-December, after all the exams are over.' And she reels off a string of names, none of which Geraldine has ever heard.

'That's all?'

'No, there's one other piece. It has slipped my mind . . . some old warhorse . . . Oh yes, "Carnival of the Animals" by Saint-Saens. It will feature two young pianists from the university, and a narrator from a youth theatre group. That's for the verses. You know . . . "The Swan can swim while sitting down, For pure conceit she takes the crown . . ." '

' ". . . She looks in the mirror over and over And claims never to have heard of Pavlova". '

'How do you know that?'

'We . . . learnt it at school.' Not quite true; she learnt it from the bit of paper with the cassette. Geraldine pretends to go back to her book to hide the eagerness in her eyes.

'Well, what do you think of the programme?'

Geraldine takes a deep breath. 'You said something before about having a kid to conduct.'

'They must have dropped that idea. All those pieces are too hard. Too many changes of tempo.'

'I could have,' mumbles Geraldine.

'Could have what?'

'Conducted the "Carnival of the Animals". I know it backwards.'

'Never, Jellybean. Two pianists to keep together? Change of tempo for every animal? They'd never take the risk.'

'I know that music,' she says stubbornly, but with less conviction. She wishes she had never opened her mouth.

The subject has evidently been dismissed. 'Ten o'clock, Jellybean. Some friends are coming for lunch. Would you go up to the bread shop for me and get some French bread? You can get an ice-block.'

Bribery, mutters Geraldine under her breath. As her mother leaves, she flings back the duvet cover angrily. Why will no one take her seriously? Only Gerald does . . . did. Most probably she'll never see him again. If he didn't play very well and hasn't been made a member of the orchestra, he will have crawled away into a hole and started teaching somewhere, up north. She is dismayed to find that her memory of him has blurred and faded like one of Mum's old photos. So has any interest or hope she might have had in the so-called youth concert. It has been dashed on yet another of her mother's famous lunch parties.

8

Spring arrives, early city spring of pink cherry blossom in front gardens on the way to school and lambs running after their mothers in the park. There is rain, too, filling the August holidays with long dark afternoons of friends visiting or visiting friends. The adults sit for hours drinking coffee, sometimes wine, talking, and laughing. Geraldine envies her mother her friends. She plays with the young children they sometimes bring or watches television with the older ones, welcoming the diversion but forgetting them the minute they drive away.

She does not really expect anything different. At school before the holidays her classmates talked of going ski-ing, flying to Fiji, Disneyland even. Sometimes she and her mother go to the pictures, or the museum, or the park. Several times they visit historic homes, big wooden echoing places where Geraldine can almost hear the living sounds of families with servants, babies, grandparents, aunties, bustle and laughter. Her heart aches a little as she thinks of their empty little flat and the one set of grandparents she has seen only twice as they are remote, in another part of the country, an expensive air flight or two days and two nights' travel by train and boat away.

Rehearsals are her one source of continuing pleasure. In the holidays there is one most mornings. Where once she was content to sit at the back and let the music come to her, now she sits nearer the front, at the right so that her mother's back is towards her and she can clearly observe the conductor's beat. Several conductors come and go but mostly it is the regular Maestro with his bald head and distant expression. He rarely seems to talk to anyone. Geraldine always keeps well clear of him. She knows that he is unmarried, lives completely for music and that the orchestra counts itself lucky that he chooses to live and work in this city rather than accept offers from elsewhere, overseas.

She has also taken to reading regularly the orchestra's schedule on the wall by the telephone and now always knows what music is being rehearsed and performed. She is not surprised when her mother announces at breakfast one morning during the second week of the school holidays, 'The ballet company's in town. Dress rehearsal at His Majesty's this morning, Jellybean. You'll enjoy that. It's *Casse Noisette – The Nutcracker*. One of the most popular of all the classical ballets, although most people know only the orchestral suite performed as a concert piece. Pity really, 'cause they never hear some of the best music.'

It starts a train of thought: her tape, that lovely celeste piece . . .

'Don't scowl, Jellybean. It'll be much more interesting than an orchestral call.'

'I'm not scowling.'

'You look so serious all the time. Sometimes I wish you played like other children,' she says, buttering toast busily.

'Like what?'

'Other children . . . Oh, I don't know . . . asking them here after school, riding a bike up and down the street . . .'

'I haven't got a bike, so how . . .'

'Well, the usual things. I suppose you spend far too much time with me, at rehearsal, sitting by yourself.'

'I don't mind.'

'Perhaps next holidays we should see about a camp or something.'

'No.'

'Wouldn't you like all the activities – swimming, cooking barbecues, sleeping in a tent, bush walks, horse riding, the concert on the last night?'

'I'd hate it. I get bossed around enough at school.'

'Well,' her mother sighs, 'why don't you ever bring a friend home from school?'

'I haven't got any friends. And there's nothing to do here.'

'Jellybean, that's not at all true. There's the tape . . .'

'No one likes my sort of music at school. They think you're a pouff if you like music. You can like rock, the top forty, that stuff . . .'

'Oh, dear. I hoped we'd got past that, this day and age.'

'And we don't have a colour telly, or heaps of Lego or skates or bikes or dress-ups or computer games or any of the other things they all seem to have at home . . .'

In the silence Geraldine sees she has gone too far. Her mother's face is like a mask.

'Whatever happened to plain old-fashioned friendship? Talking, sharing secrets. . . Well, I've got to be at the theatre by 9.15, Geraldine. You'd better get dressed.'

The silence continues in the car. Geraldine stares out at the rush-hour traffic making its way into the city.

'I hope we're going to make it,' says her mother as they sit motionless in a long queue. By the time they are moving again and the Mini is parked, Geraldine's watch has passed nine.

Her mother slams the car door, runs around to the other side, grabs the cello and her music case.

'It's twelve past! Jellybean, I must dash. You can come on slowly if you like. You know the way, don't you?'

'Yes.' Does she?

'Down those steps over there, straight down that little steep street, turn left at Queen Street. The theatre arcade is just along a bit.'

‘I know.’ She doesn’t really, but she remembers how upset her mother was once before when they were late. There was a frigid pause in which the conductor waited for her to get out her cello, dig the spike into the floor, tighten the knob on the bow. It was the same at school when the headmaster made people stand up for whispering in assembly and sent them pink-faced from the hall. Geraldine always suffered for them and she dreaded it ever happening to her.

‘See you.’ Her mother’s face bends to the car window. ‘Meet you in the break . . . Careful crossing the road . . .’

Geraldine, still in the back seat, watches her cross the road and disappear through an archway. Slowly, relishing this unusual chance to move at her own pace, she climbs out of the car. Everything is grey: the pavement, the sky, the harbour just visible at the bottom of the wide street. Even the air feels damp and grey. Waiting for a break in the traffic, she pulls her parka around her. It is last year’s and feels uncomfortably short and cold around her bottom and wrists. In her haste, her mother has forgotten to give her money for the parking meter.

The steps below the archway are steep and narrow. She wonders how many musicians, hurrying late for a rehearsal or performance, have tripped. Hugging the dark stone wall, she goes down carefully. At the foot of the stairs, two narrow lanes meet. She pauses, confused. Behind her a sign saying ‘Gentlemen’ marks a door disappearing under the road. Starting forward, she trips and falls onto her knees. A car brakes hard. Its driver, winding down the window, shouts angrily, ‘Do you want to get yourself killed?’ as he drives off.

At the bottom of the narrow lane, Queen Street’s cars and buses flash by. Only when she reaches the corner does she notice that her knees are stinging and that there are pinpricks of blood on them. Had Mum said right or left?

Trying to blink away the tears, she looks up and down the busy street but can see no signs that say 'Theatre'. She turns the first way her body thinks of, which is right, uphill. She passes a cinema entrance, even at this hour full of mothers and kids queuing for the latest school holiday film. In the window of a bride shop, a bride doll, head to toe in lace and frills, gazes out blankly. Next are traffic lights. The 'theatre arcade' her mother had spoken of is nowhere to be seen.

Everyone waits at the lights for the 'Cross Now' sign, except for one skinny man in ragged jeans and headband who waits for nothing. Geraldine stares at the pavement, counting the dried circles of chewing gum. Perhaps the theatre is in the next block up? Swept along by the tide of people, she finds that guess to be wrong again. She passes many shops until she comes to a chocolate shop with its windows displaying gold and silver mounds of chocolates. Inside there is carpet on the floor, and a rich atmosphere of chocolate and money. She remembers a fifty cent piece in her jeans pocket, and fingers it regretfully when the woman behind the counter tells her that her first choice, a tiny rabbit in shiny red paper, is 'Ninety cents, dear.' For that? She tries again. Those loose chocolates. 'Four fifty a kilo,' which means nothing. How many for fifty cents? The woman sniffs, picks out two or three with her tongs and puts them on the scales. Four, it seems. Geraldine is about to say okay, when the woman switches on an instant smile for a man standing next to her, a twenty dollar note in his hand. She serves him, all teeth and eyelashes and sir, and then another man; then a woman who spends several minutes on the forms needed to be filled in for bankcards.

By this time Geraldine is more intrigued than angry. She looks about her: perhaps she really has become totally invisible, for not one of the adults has given the slightest hint that she, Jellybean, exists, that she is standing on this patch of carpet, her hand holding this fifty cent piece on this glass-topped counter, her breath clouding this corner of the glass.

After the fifth customer has handed over her money and taken her gift-wrapped parcel, Geraldine has had enough. The smell of chocolate has become suffocating. She dives back into the real world of ordinary people, cars, buses, seen through a prickling warm blur of tears. I will, she thinks, take my fifty cents elsewhere. It is a good expression, one her mother uses, implying disdain.

Without her noticing, anger has turned her feet down hill. She goes through the traffic lights and past the small lane leading up to the archway above the steps. A little further down she stops suddenly in front of a billboard announcing the ballet company's season. She has remembered the theatre arcade for which she has been looking. It is a long covered alleyway, with small shops on either side. At the end, behind a padlocked iron grille, are some steps leading up into the theatre. She has forgotten how unglamorous and shabby it all looks by day without the people there, without the hum of a gathering audience.

Today only two or three people are lingering. The shops look empty and the stage door beside the staircase looks a forbidding barrier. From inside she can hear, very faintly, the sound of the orchestra playing.

The stage door is the only way in. Perhaps she can just hang around outside until her mother has finished? She could go for another walk up Queen Street but one glance back towards the street finishes that idea. Boring, *boring, boring,* she mutters, and takes a deep breath before marching through the Stage Door as though she owns the place.

9

Inside the door, the sensation of having walked into another world, out of time, is so real that for a few moments Geraldine has to stand quite still. Then she notices a strange but not unpleasant smell. The music, suddenly much louder, is a waltz in three-four time, which her hand quite by itself begins to beat. Above her head are soft rhythmic thuds: dancers' feet. Luckily the chair by the stage door is empty, with no stern man there to ask her to explain herself or tick off her name on a clipboard.

Ahead is a short passageway, the entrance to this spaceship and nothing glamorous. Paint is peeling off the concrete walls. If anything it is colder and damper than the draughty arcade outside. Her brief moment of bravado has vanished as quickly as it came, leaving a dull anger at her mother for rushing off and leaving her. Some vague memory of past visits – one, two years ago? – tells her that the way down to the auditorium is first of all up that short flight of stairs, and not down those others into the narrow hallway of Alice-in-Wonderland closed doors.

Turning the corner at the top of the stairs, she recognizes that she is actually very close to the stage. Her step falters. Through painted canvas scenery, spotlights on stands or hanging from above, and a confusion of people – stage hands tiptoeing about, waiting dancers continually on the move to try and keep warm – she can see a stage brilliantly alive.

There are men and women dressed as if for a party, a number of children, and a servant girl. At the back of the stage is a Christmas tree so beautiful with tiny crystal candles, silver parcels, and stars the colours of fire and frost that it makes her gasp. It is a family gathering, Christmas Day, and a party is indeed in progress. The children, maybe ten or eleven of them, are receiving presents – dolls for the girls; drums, whistles, and guns for the boys. The girls look doll-like in pastel muslin dresses, pantaloons and ringlets, porcelain faces. The boys are in formal suits of weird colours: mustard, pink, apple green. There is some fooling about, some teasing of the girls and consequent reprimands, but it is all in good humour.

Despite herself, forgetting that she is trying to get down into the audience where she should be, Geraldine finds herself sidling along the side wall to get a better view. One man is clearly to be avoided at all costs. Bristling with earphones, walkie-talkie, clipboard and a microphone into which he occasionally murmurs directions, he is controlling the smooth running of the performance and misses little, onstage or off. But even he has not seen her yet, she feels sure. She steps carefully past an octopus of wires, switches and plugs, and tucks herself into a little nook behind him. From there she can see most of the front part of the stage.

A visitor has arrived, some sort of magician in a great swirling cape of black with moons and stars on it. His 'puppets' perform. There is a couple in masks, and a tin soldier in green with painted red cheeks and jerky movements. Geraldine is beginning to relax and enjoy the party as though she is sitting safely in her proper seat, when the magician produces a carved wooden doll. He gives it to one particular girl in pink muslin. A fight breaks out, less good humoured this time. The boys want it. The adults intervene. The squabble continues. Geraldine protests silently: how *can* they, when they have all that? The toy – she can see it now, a wooden man, a soldier perhaps, painted, rather ugly but immensely desirable – gets broken.

The nastiest boy is pleased. The girl is so heart-broken

that Geraldine finds herself forgetting it is only a stage and only a ballet she is watching. There are tears in her eyes for the girl and for the family Christmas she will never know, squabbles and all. Finally, when the girl has sadly hospitalized her flawed wooden man in a cot and the party is over and the lights grow dim leaving only the Christmas tree glowing softly at the back, Geraldine can bear it no longer. The music has begun to worry her.

The door down to the auditorium is half-closed. There is no way out except back the way she came. She begins to move through the muddle of furniture and props and ropes and lights, and has almost made it to the exit when she comes face to face with a mouse, very much in a hurry. Behind this mouse are others, a nightmare army of them, it seems. Some are closely followed by women still doing up the zips at the back of the costumes. These are the same children, doing a quick-change into mice.

Geraldine side-steps, trips over a wire, and knocks down a spare spotlight standing against the wall. The crash can be clearly heard over the music as grotesque sounds of metal and broken glass form a mismatched duet with a single bell chiming. Shrivelled against the wall, Geraldine sees heads turn but she is saved by the general flurry of people in the confined space, by the shadows, and by a curtain hanging down the side wall. As the man with the headphone starts towards the disturbance, she slips behind the curtain.

Sounds of hoarse whispers – 'Keep away from the glass,' 'Over here, walk over *here*' – mingle with the music which has become menacing and sullen. Flutes nibble at the air; some sort of lower woodwind, a bassoon perhaps, gnaws away at her shame and terror. The music grows louder by the bar, so perfectly matching her growing fear of being discovered that she finds herself pressing harder and harder against the cold concrete at her back. Still the music grows, as though being pumped up by a giant; louder and higher, with the violins reaching upwards and upwards until she feels the theatre and her head with it are going to explode.

There is a sudden change, to flutes so slippery and chilling that a shiver runs down her spine. Then a rifle shot. That's it, she thinks. I'm not staying here one minute longer. Battle-lines are clearly forming. Without bothering to poke her head around the curtain to check if she will be seen, she fights her way out from behind it. In her one desperate look at the stage, she sees that the Christmas tree is now twice the size it was. She flees.

It would have been far more sensible, as things turned out, if she had fled through the stage door and out into the real world, a world where trees stay the same size and music cannot reach into your heart and make you forget who and where you are, and send you half off your head. But her frantic feet take her down both flights of stairs into the Alice corridor.

Here the music, though still audible and still fighting a battle to the death, has lost its immediate power over her. The air is damp and stuffy, the smell she noticed earlier is stronger, the atmosphere more like a dungeon. She runs down one passageway after another until she reaches a set of small steps leading up to a locked door: the end of the line.

She sits for a long time, huddled up, needing the solitude to recover. Not until the battle reaches its climax, and the music changes completely to a soothing victorious sound of harp and strings does she begin to feel in control of herself again. She hears flutes again, but this time they are fragile and delicate. Then there is the surprising sound of women's voices in a long flowing melody, so unusual that she wants to hear it better.

As she retraces her steps, Geraldine passes the Alice doors, some half open. They are, she sees now, empty dressing-rooms, messy places full of clothes, mirrors, chairs, bright lights. On each doorway is pinned a piece of cardboard with three, four or five names marked on it. One in particular has something about it. She pauses, and pushes the door open a little further. There are child-size shoes on the floor, a Miss Piggy doll propped on one side of the cluttered dressing table, a teddy bear on the other and children's clothes hang around the walls. An arch of lightbulbs around the mirror makes the whole room almost unbearably bright. There is also a heater on, which draws her inside.

Standing in front of the single red bar, which toasts the back of her knees, Geraldine realizes she is panting slightly. The naked sound of breaking glass still rasps through her head: glass, dancers' feet. Oh, what has she done? Yet she is fairly sure that in the shadows no one had actually seen her face or been close enough to recognize her. She looks at herself in the mirror: big scared eyes, boring face, mouse hair all over, parka sleeves half-way up her arms. Not a pretty sight.

So far she seems to have spent the whole morning trying to find a place to go. Even here, in someone else's dressing-room, she is far from comfortable. Yet short of sitting on the stairs outside, where else *can* she go until the interval?

As the feeling of panic slowly recedes, Geraldine begins to take in the clutter of the dressing-room. She decides to play the jellybean game, a game she has often played before in strange rooms belonging to her mother's friends. What sort of person lives here? Count the clues.

On the floor are several pairs of smallish boots and sneakers, brand new. She notices this particularly, as hers are always old and scruffy. On the hangers above are jeans, also new-looking and of an expensive brand, a frilly blouse, sweat shirts with names in big letters across the front, parkas, woolly hats. All are very neatly hung up. Either the girls who own them are very tidy or they have tidy mothers to do it for them. There are also two or three big bags stuffed with goodness-knows-what, but her game does not extend to looking in other people's bags. On other hangers are costumes, such pretty long dresses that the game permits her to stroke the lace on the neck and finger the frills. One is white with a tartan sash. The materials are coarser than they first appeared.

She has just wandered over to the dressing-table and sat herself in front of it, and is smelling one of the tubes of make-up (a stronger version of the strange smell), when she hears voices, clatter and footsteps. So absorbed has she been in the jellybean game that she hasn't noticed the music has stopped and a man's voice can be heard over a crackling loudspeaker. Before she has a chance to realize, and to get out of the chair and out of the dressing-room, she sees reflected in the mirror two girls standing in the doorway. Caught!

They stare at her curiously for a moment, before a third face joins them from behind. A mother. The expression on this face is far from friendly.

Geraldine puts down the tube and springs off the chair, knocking it flying in the process.

'Oh, I'm sorry. . . I. . .' She bends to pick up the chair. When she straightens, the mother is inside the door, demanding, 'Who are you?'

'Um . . . Geraldine . . .'

'What are you doing in here?'

Geraldine looks at the two girls. One is a skinny grey mouse, holding the mask under her arm. Her eyes mirror the hostility of the mother. The other, a little taller, Geraldine recognizes as the owner of the wooden doll, in her pink muslin dress. Her expression is more curious than hostile.

'I. . . I. . .' But the words can't get past her tongue.

'Street kid, I suppose. Nothing better to do than sneak into warm places around the city and steal. School holidays, no father, mother on the DPB, sponging on tax-payers' hard-earned money. *I* know.'

The injustice of what she has said leaves Geraldine speechless. She stares into the cold eyes which are shiny and hard and surrounded by elaborate shadows of make-up.

'You don't look like a street kid to me,' says the older girl, sitting down on one of the chairs.

'Yes she does,' puts in the mouse, but Geraldine has had enough and by this time has sidled her way around to the door.

'Let me look in your pockets. . . I wouldn't mind betting . . .'

Geraldine is not stopping to take any more of this. She moves out the door and dashes up the nearest flight of stairs and around the corner, only to find herself flattened against the wall by a flash flood of people. Some are mice and their mothers, some the adults from the Christmas party, some are stage-hands in jeans carrying things. There is a large group of dancers in white tutus, their faces shiny with sweat and make-up, eyes heavy with tiredness and false eyelashes so thick that Geraldine wonders how they ever manage to keep their eyes open. Seen close up, these girls look thin and used to hard work.

Rather than fight against this noisy flood, Geraldine can only go with it. The more people there are about, the less likely she is to be noticed. Now she finds herself washed out into a large open space. From the noises above she guesses it is right under the stage. It is full of people, some dancers moving through to other dressing-rooms, but mostly, she sees now with a sinking heart, members of the orchestra. They are climbing through a low door from the orchestra pit, holding their instruments carefully in front of them. Those players already there are drinking tea. The walls are lined with instrument cases, big and small.

She had never imagined that this pokey, grubby, low-ceilinged and very cold dungeon would be the orchestra's meeting-place. It doesn't match up, somehow. None of this scruffy, smelly backstage does.

Geraldine hesitates, and ducks behind an ironing board, taking refuge in a rack of costumes. She does not feel like coping with her mother. She shouldn't be here at all; she should be sitting quietly out in the audience, reading her book. Instead she has knocked over a lamp near the stage and probably caused untold panic, not to mention cut feet. But there was one good thing: the music had not stopped. She had not interrupted a rehearsal.

One quick glance around the room has told her that her mother has not yet come through from the pit. Now, during the break, would be her best opportunity to try yet again to make it up to the auditorium. She might, though, be recognized by the headphone man, whose corner she will have to pass. She decides it's a risk she'll have to take.

Before she can move, two things happen. First, the rack of costumes close to her head rustles.

'Hey. Geraldine!'

Who in this place knows her name, apart from her mother?

'I've been looking everywhere for you. Come on.' It is the older of the two girls, still in her pink dress, taking her hand and tugging her away from the wall. 'Jenny's ghastly mother has gone.'

And just as she is being led away from the crowded room the second thing happens, so briefly that she is left wondering if she imagined it. She sees, stooping to come through the low door from the pit, not her mother as she feared, but a bearded man. She sees him only in profile as he straightens up, then her view is obscured by two large men carrying French horns.

'Come on.' The hand has tugged her back into the corridor and along towards the dressing-rooms. Her rescuer shuts the door. 'There. I thought you might have run away for good. I wouldn't have blamed you. Your mother needn't have said all that,' she says sternly to the younger girl, obviously Jenny, who is now sitting in front of the dressing-table, still dressed in her grey mouse body tights and brushing her long thin hair.

Jenny opens her mouth to speak, but the older girl has already turned back to Geraldine and gets in first.

'Your name is Geraldine, right. And I bet you're not a street kid.'

Confused with the speed of events and the shock that, after all these months, it really was her friend Gerald she has just seen, Geraldine stares back blankly.

'Well, whatever she is, I don't like people fiddling with my things,' comes a pompous little voice from the chair. Geraldine ignores her.

'No. Of course I'm not,' she says indignantly. 'I'm supposed to be out in the audience. My mother's in the orchestra.'

'Well, what were you doing in here then?'

'Oh, be quiet, Jenny,' says the pink muslin girl. 'You're as bad as your mother.' She turns back to Geraldine. 'Bored out of your mind, I bet, with all those snowflakes. Decided to go for a walk.'

'Snowflakes?'

'In the last scene, after the transformation.'

Geraldine, lost, can only smile.

'I'm Susie. That's Jenny. She's one of the other children at the party, then a mouse, then a bonbon in the second act. I'm Clara.'

'The one with the broken doll?'

'The nutcracker? Yep, that's me.'

There is a moment's awkwardness. Neither of them quite seems to know what to say next. Geraldine, in her old jeans and too-small parka, feels shabby and colourless beside Susie in her stage dress.

'Sit down. Jenny won't mind,' Susie says cheerfully. 'Her mother's gone off to have a cup of tea or a word with somebody about something. She's always going off to see somebody about something.'

'Not complain about me, I hope,' says Geraldine quickly.

'What for? Oh you mean, a strange body in the dressing-room. Well, it's not the end of the world, is it? No, much more important than that.'

Like knocking over spotlights near the stage, Geraldine thinks, but she's not going to admit that to anyone unless she has to.

'Like the music in the first act being too fast,' continues Suzie breezily. 'Or too slow. Or something.'

'Well, so it was.'

'Jenny, it was exactly like it has been every other time,' says Susie with quiet patience.

'That conductor doesn't know what she's doing.'

Geraldine is not sure if she's heard correctly.

Susie's patience is clearly running out. 'How can you *say* that?'

'My mother says she's just a jumped-up pianist.'

'Your mother says far too much, if you ask me,' Susie remarks pointedly.

'My mother says that the other conductor, the man, is much better and that Frederica whatever-her-name-is should be dismissed before she has the chance to ruin a performance. Women shouldn't try to be conductors, she says.'

'Your mother doesn't know what she's talking about. It makes no difference whatsoever. You can't tell when you're dancing which conductor it is, unless you actually look down. The music's the same.'

Jenny, now sulky, goes on silently brushing her hair.

'Go on, admit it. You *can't* tell, and one of these days. . .' Susie turns towards Geraldine, 'Little Jenny here is going to realize that not everything her mother says is the gospel truth.'

Geraldine is busy with her own thoughts. There must be two conductors for this ballet season and one of them is female and is conducting the dress rehearsal this morning. Why didn't her mother, her very own mother, tell her? And another thing, why didn't she tell her about Gerald being in the orchestra?

The day is beginning to prove interesting.

'Tell me about the conductor,' says Geraldine. 'The female one.' In a few minutes she might finally be able to get into the audience where she can watch this unusual lady in action.

Susie shrugs. 'I don't know all that much. She's tall and skinny, about thirty. She *is* a pianist, and a very good one. Done lots of musicals, been on television. I think this is her first time with the ballet orchestra, just for the matinees.'

'Well, she has to start somewhere.'

'Not on us,' Jenny mutters.

'Why not?' demands Geraldine, warming up.

'Don't forget, Jenny,' interrupts Susie, 'that this is your first time on the big stage.'

'So?' Jenny throws her hairbrush into the clutter on the dressing table.

'But not yours?' says Geraldine to Susie, forgetting the conductor for a moment.

'Is it that obvious?'

'Well, I . . .' Geraldine hesitates, not sure how her question has been taken. But the older girl is smiling.

'Do I look like an old hand? That's what my mother calls me. This is my third production.'

'Is she somewhere around here too?' Geraldine is off mothers today, and fully intends getting out of the dressing-room very soon, before any more of them find her.

'My mother won't even come to my ballet lessons. She refuses to be a ballet mum. She says this is my scene. She's happy to come and enjoy the performance like anyone else.'

'You must be very good at ballet,' says Geraldine, greatly impressed.

'Yes, well, I've been learning for years and years and years, since I was five. Twice a week. Exams and that, every year. But I'm getting a bit tall. Some of the real dancers aren't much taller than me.'

'Are you going to be a real dancer?'

Susie looks thoughtful. 'I want to. But it's hard even to get into the national dance school. Actually, I'd like to do music at university. Or be a teacher.'

How amazing, to be so good at two things, to have so many choices, to talk so . . . confidently, Geraldine thinks. Yet Susie is not so very much older than herself, maybe one, two years.

'What do you play?' Geraldine asks.

'Violin. Oh, yes. You said your mother's in the orchestra. What does she play?'

'Cello.'

'You play something? Are you going to be a musician, too?'

'Only piano, sort of.'

To her relief, before she can answer the second part of the question, a bell rings somewhere and she hears voices outside in the corridor.

'That's ten minutes to curtain up. Time to think about the next bit.' Geraldine can tell that Susie's attention has shifted away from her. She is looking at her image critically in the mirror. Then she jumps up and starts rummaging in her bag. 'You going out front to watch?'

Geraldine is already on her feet. The last thing she wants is another confrontation with Jenny's ghastly mum. Anyway, she has some investigating to do. 'I'm going.'

'See you.' Their eyes meet briefly in the mirror. Geraldine opens the door to find the very person she never wants to meet again.

'Excuse me. I'm just leaving,' she says to the legs and high heels.

Jenny's mum advances a fraction, threateningly.

'I thought I told you to leave the premises.'

'It's all right, Mrs Taylor. I asked her in,' says a calm voice behind. Taylor? Another grotty Mrs Taylor. The town seems to be full of them.

'You had no right to do that, Susan.'

'Oh, I think I did.' Geraldine is astonished by the sweetness of her new friend's voice. 'Her mother plays in the orchestra so it's *quite* all right. She's just going back out front to watch the second act.'

Geraldine now has enough courage to raise her head and meet Mrs Taylor's glare. Behind the careful make-up are angry eyes, the eyes of someone who spends her time arguing and fighting with people. But momentarily defeated, Mrs Taylor steps back. Geraldine sweeps past her and down a corridor. Only when she turns the corner, does she find she has chosen the wrong way again. She waits a moment or two, then returns the way she has come. There are plenty of people going in and out of dressing-rooms, but no Mrs Taylor, so she saunters back past the half-open door.

Susie is sitting at her dressing-table, doing her hair. Mrs Taylor is bent over Jenny, now in a spotty costume, doing something to her make-up. Only Susie sees Geraldine in the mirror. She winks.

10

The problem is as before: how to find her way through the rabbit-warren and eventually poke her head up where she should be, out in the audience. Alert for hostile mothers and pouncing stage managers, Geraldine adopts a purposeful walk but recognizing the entrance to the tea-drinking area, she falters. Her mother she doesn't feel like coping with – or Gerald, if it was indeed him. A reluctance has taken hold of her as far as he is concerned. She wants to watch him play, and to renew their friendship in her own good time. She feels hurt that he has not sent a message to her through her mother. If it wasn't for her, she thinks bitterly, he might never have done that audition.

She turns and finds another staircase to go up, then a second one, more familiar, and is relieved to find herself once more in the area near the stage where she first watched Susie dancing. The curtain is closed, and the stage is busy with people moving scenery and dancers warming up, grinding the toes of their pointed shoes into a box of white powder. The glass has evidently been completely cleared away, for there is no sign of anyone with brooms. This time the headphone man is over the other side of the stage, and Geraldine sees that the way down into the audience is at last clear.

The auditorium is in semi-darkness, with only the footlights and the lights of the orchestra's music stands creating a glow up onto the folds of the red curtain and around the pit itself. There is sufficient light to reveal a few people scattered about the stalls, a group of children talking noisily and over there a knot of women, ballet mums, best avoided. Geraldine leans against the wall for a moment, relieved at having made it. Most of the musicians are still backstage but there are already some woodwind players piping away in the pit, several violinists, and the timpani player bent low over his drums, tuning them. Her task now is to find the best place to watch this extraordinary person, this conductor who is female and thirty. Also she wants to see if her vision of Gerald was real. She wanders up the side aisle and across the back. One or two faces glance at her and look away. Then some habit, or some instinct, draws her back down the other side of the theatre towards the orchestra.

Perhaps it is the darkness, or the shadows; perhaps it is something about this day which is turning out to be a little crazy, but before she has time to think about what she is doing, Geraldine finds herself crouching by the brass rail dividing the orchestra pit from the audience. She lifts up the little curtain.

The musicians already in the pit are on the other side or far too preoccupied with their instruments to notice her. She looks down and sees right below her a strange little piano. She can even read the name of the music on the illuminated stand: 'Dance of the Sugar Plum Fairy'. Of course. The famous celeste. So intrigued is she by this discovery that she pulls aside the low curtain and slides down into the pit.

Frozen in the shadows beside the celeste and a forest of music stands, chairs, cellos and double basses, Geraldine catches her breath. Surely someone must have heard the thud of her feet as she landed. Slowly she raises her head. Her audacity today appalls her. So does the realization that she is now trapped, for two more violinists are taking their seats nearby. Now comes a cellist, one of the other women players, followed by two double-bass players. It is only a matter of time before both her mother and Gerald come through that little door.

Crouched on her haunches, taking infinite care not to touch or knock anything, Geraldine slides noiselessly into the farthest corner of the pit, behind the last double-bass stool. She cannot go any further or make herself any smaller.

What a stupid situation to end up in! Stuck for the rest of the morning or about to be stumbled over by a double-bass player pushing back his stool. Discovery, now or later, will mean instant shame. She can imagine only too clearly the orchestra stopped and watching, the dancers looking down, as she climbs out, the icy silence – and her mother's anger.

Then she giggles, deciding her situation has its funny side. From here she can see the conductor's rostrum and now the conductor, flicking over the pages of the score. The reflected light gives her face ghostly unreal shadows, but Geraldine can see enough: a bony clever face, long hair. She takes up the white baton, and talks to the violinists nearby.

Gerald arrives. As she fears, he takes the last cello seat, the one nearest her. He gives no sign of noticing anything unusual. She watches his easy familiar movements of preparation; tightening the bow, digging the cello spike into the floor, checking the music. He does not interrupt his concentration with idle chatter to the players around him, but only pauses to let the last double-bass and celeste player squeeze past.

Through the noise the oboe note calls. The orchestra tunes and waits. In the silence Geraldine realizes that one seat among the cellos has remained empty – her mother's.

What breaks the tension is not the music, but a loud male voice amplified to booming level.

'Would Geraldine Waite please go immediately to the stage door. If Geraldine Waite is in the house, would she go immediately to the stage door where her mother is waiting for her.' The microphone clicks off. There is another long silence.

Geraldine, rigid with shame, has her eyes tightly closed. She does not see the players raise their instruments, or the tiny red light glow beside the conductor's music. She hears only, through hands cupped over her ears to blot out that voice, the music begin around her. For now she has remembered; she was supposed to meet her mother during the break. Her mother would have absolutely no idea where she is. Instead of sitting there playing her cello, she is pacing up and down outside the stage door in that empty arcade. Oh Mum . . . I'm sorry . . . I never meant . . .

The music soars above her, with the harpist on the other side of the pit accompanying a flowing violin melody and all the cellos and double-basses pizzicato-ing away. It begins to work its familiar magic and the uncontrollable blush which she knows from past experience will have coloured her face a hot pink is starting to subside. She can even open her eyes.

The curtain has gone up, but from her low position in the corner, Geraldine can see only the front part of the stage. Oh well, she thinks, being stuck, I may as well make the best of it. She can at least watch the conductor, who is smiling, clearly delighting in every moment, her eyes watching both players and dancers.

Susie comes into view, walking and looking every inch a dancer. She is escorted by the magician, and seated like an honoured guest on some sort of low throne directly above her on the extreme left of the stage. Geraldine shrinks further, if possible, into her corner. It has occurred to her that if she can see Susie so clearly, then perhaps Susie has only to look down into the pit to see her. She does not know if she can see past the footlights.

The music becomes familiar, comforting her whirling

thoughts like an old friend and keeping her mind off her mother's wrath to come. She has conducted some of these pieces at home: the Arabian dance, steamy music of low woodwind; the Chinese dance, the piccolo shrill over bassoons; the furious Russian dance with its breathless ending. As each dance finishes there is a deathly hush while the dancers rehearse their bows at the front of the stage. An audience would be clapping now.

The final plucked chords of the 'Dance of the Toy Flutes' have just finished when Geraldine feels something move against her left leg. She gasps, but has enough sense left to cut off most of the sound with her hand. Every hair on her leg is standing straight up. The other hand feels down, to what? – a rat, mouse, cat?

She sees a small cat, black like Quaver, slinking off behind the celeste player's stool.

Her intake of breath seemed as loud in the silence as if she had stood up and shouted to the whole theatre, 'Look it's me, Jellybean,' but there is no reaction. She curls herself into the smallest ball she can possibly make of herself. She is reduced to two big eyes watching for heads to turn: Gerald's, the conductor's. Another dance begins, the harp again.

Perhaps Gerald's head turns just slightly a minute or so later, during a pause in his music. She can't be sure for by then she has become a little ball of anger.

Oh, Geraldine has never felt so angry, so hot with rage. She is glowing red with the heat of her anger. How come? she thinks. Just how come I've got into this position? Mother and her stupid orchestra, that's what. Always traipsing off to rehearsal calls, playing her stupid cello after school, holidays, nights on end.

Everyone in this theatre has a reason for being here but me, she thinks bitterly. They make beautiful music, dance to perfection. I just have to keep out of the way.

Even watching the conductor and feeling part of the orchestra now gives her no pleasure at all. Whatever made her think she could do that: stand there, in control, with everyone watching, so sure of herself, when really she's nothing but a nuisance. And at this very moment, her mother is probably at the stage door more angry than Geraldine has ever seen her. 'Geraldine,' she would say, 'how could you? How *could* you?

11

Geraldine realizes she is actually jealous of her mother's cello. Very well, she thinks, I have reason to be. And if I am going to be a nuisance, I may as well do a good job.

A cat, even a small one, could mean a mouse. Not a silly dressed-up mouse like that silly Jenny prancing around the stage, but a real small warm slithering mouse. I'm going to buy one from the pet shop and next time I have to come to a boring rehearsal, I'll let it go.

Geraldine closes her eyes. I'll be that mouse, she thinks . . . I'll start right here, by the double-bass player's foot which will look quite as big as Mum's Mini. There's the spike of the double-bass stretching up into the dark, as big as a telegraph pole, and when I touch it with my paw I find it humming as the player above me saws away, making giants' music. Now I'm running through an endless landscape of legs. Chair legs, music stand legs, people legs.

Feet is what I'm after.

Men's feet aren't so good for a mouse. They are encased in black leather or running shoes. I could go up and over their ankles, in the gap between shoes and trouser bottoms, but I'm not sure how good my paws are at hanging on to those steep little hills.

Ha! Over there is the perfect foot – plump, female, and bare, because the violin player to whom it belongs has slipped off her shoes.

Up and over, as fast as I can. The toes curl. The foot is raised several inches off the ground. The toes of the other foot clench and stay clenched, I note with satisfaction.

Now, peering round the edge of someone's handbag,

I decide I'll let my victim stew for a bit. I sit on my haunches and listen, conducting with the tip of my tail. I'm feeling better already. Oh, the toes have relaxed. I'll try another up-and-over, this time pausing – yuk – to take a tiny nibble at the big toe.

The foot jerks into mid-air. I'm thrown off, but I land on all fours and scurry off into a corner. The music continues, but the violinist is whispering something to the man next door. Feet get moved around a bit, a face peers down. Well, well, so the owner of those fat female feet isn't too scared of mice. Or is she rather more scared of the ultimate humiliation, interrupting a rehearsal? The feet are back on the floor, but tensed. I'll try again.

This time I dig teeth firmly into the big toe, through pantyhose and all. Wonderful. As I pick myself up and dash off, I hear a magnificent disturbance. The violinist, giving a tiny scream and jerking both feet off the ground, has toppled backwards. She can't go far, just enough to upset the music stands of the players behind and land in their startled laps. Bits of music float downwards.

The music continues, although I can hear some odd sounds from the violinists. Once more, for luck. I take a deep breath and run as far and as fast as I can, right over to the other side of the pit, keeping close to the wall all the way. Here is a lady who plays the French horn; no friend of mine, nor of my mother either, I know. She's always complaining. I know she can't stand children, and I bet she can't stand mice either, for all her hearty ways. She might even think I'm a rat with this mouthful. Bony ankle, encased in sock. Double yuk.

I've forgotten one thing. As I sit on my haunches wiping my front paws, listening with great satisfaction to the commotion above, I catch the gleam of two gold eyes just as the cat launches himself into the air.

At this point I will decide that being a mouse is not

my thing at all. But the scene is not yet finished; I'll simply reappear, like Superman in a place too hot to handle, in a seat just behind all the children watching the rehearsal. I'll be myself, but invisible.

Now I can see the stage completely. The Sugar Plum Fairy and her prince are doing a slow intricate duet, with many turns and lifts and arabesques. If the dancers have noticed anything amiss with the orchestra, they are too professional to show it. Their heads are held high, their smiles as fixed as ever. They dance to the gallery.

But the children in front of me are watching the orchestra with interest, tittering slightly. The fat violinist is back determinedly playing, a wild look in her eyes. I sit on the back of my chair, to get a better view. I see that the poor lady is actually squatting with some difficulty on her chair. Behind her the three violinists whose stands were knocked flying are still trying to sort out their music. One other woman player is crouched on her chair. Gerald plays on. No doubt my mother would too, if she were there. Nothing would stop her playing her cello.

On the right side of the pit the French horn has gone into a sort of faint and is being propped up by a second French horn, while a third plays on, casting despairing looks at his colleagues. A trombone player is standing up, waving his trombone, and shouting something about unions at someone in the circle above. Two flutes, one clarinet and one bassoon have also taken to their chairs, kneeling or squatting or cross-legged.

Still the orchestra plays on.

And still the dancing continues, two performers on the huge stage, perfection in slow motion. The music is building to a grand climax, the timpani is in full cry. Again I've forgotten the cat. No doubt confused by the commotion in the pit he leaps out, but lands on the top of the timpani and gets himself knocked on the head as he skids past. 'Oh my God,' shouts the timpani player, surveying the stunned animal lying before him. Throwing his sticks in the air, he stands, in a towering rage, waving his fist and joining the trombone player in shouting up at the circle.

Serve you right, I cry.

I am laughing so much it is painful. Then suddenly it occurs to me that the conductor might not be enjoying all this at all.

Her first time with the ballet company, Susie had said. It might be her last. She is conducting as though her life depends on it, but the music has a desperate quality, as though the whole orchestra is being tuned upwards. Now the dancers are showing signs of unease; there is the occasional glance downwards at the conductor for reassurance. One pirouette is so off balance that for one dreadful moment I think the ballerina is going to topple off her pointe altogether.

No! Geraldine opens her eyes and blinks herself back to reality. No!! You can't trifle with something so precious, so perfect. She is quivering all over as the music reaches its pinnacle of sound, with trumpets, timpani and the entire orchestra filling the theatre. And when the end comes, and in the echoing hush the two dancers take their bows, Geraldine finds her eyes full of tears partly because the music is so beautiful and partly because that insignificant creature called Geraldine has messed everything up.

Her legs are stiff, her bottom is numb, she means nothing to anyone, not even Gerald who she thought was her first real friend. Her mother's anger doesn't bear thinking about.

Flutes are being played now, fast and delicate. Geraldine has her head on her knees so she does not see the celeste player fidget with her music and adjust her stool. The hands are opened and closed, the fingers limbered up, then they wait on the small keyboard. Geraldine hears only the notes of crystal close by, like fairies hammering tiny bells of ice. The music creates an impossible yearning in her. She wants, she wants . . . what is it she *wants* so much? To make that music, all this music, herself? Now she lifts her head and sits erect so that she can see the conductor more clearly. She listens hard to the music, and notes with interest that the ending is quite different from the tape music she knows so well. The fingers on the keyboard ripple like sunlight on water, faster and faster, to a brilliant ending.

In her exultation, she almost claps. The conductor, from closely watching the ballerina, turns and shoots a quick smile at the celeste player. Then, while the dancer above curtseys to the silent theatre, the conductor looks back again, sharply, past the celeste.

Geraldine knows that she has been seen.

She waits, head lowered, for the voice which will interrupt the rehearsal, throw her out of the pit and out of the theatre in disgrace.

It never comes. The music begins yet again, the end of the pas de deux, followed by a big waltz with all the dancers back on the stage, the Arabians, the Chinese, the Russians, the bonbons, the flowers and the fairies and the Sugar Plum ballerina and her prince, and in the middle of it all, Susie, the star. There is even some more celeste and an exquisite soft coda of bells and pizzicato while the dancers melt away and the stage grows dark, but Geraldine is too churned up inside to respond any more. Eventually the curtain drops, then rises again immediately. Tired dancers stand flat-footed about the stage, Susie amongst them, listening to a man's voice from the circle.

The orchestra is thanked and begins to leave. The conductor leans wearily over her rostrum, then Geraldine sees her head turn slowly in her direction. She has remembered that pale face down in the corner! But she doesn't say anything or haul her out. Just looks. Geraldine's eyes drop and she feels herself blushing.

The man's voice drones on. The headphone man comes out from his corner on the right-hand side of the stage to answer questions. The dancers continue to stand about, hands on hips, panting less now.

Most of the orchestra, including the conductor, have gone. When, oh when will I ever get out of here? Geraldine thinks in despair. There is still one cellist in his seat, slowly packing up his music and it's the last person she wants to see – that is, other than her mother.

Suddenly, she's had enough of hiding, of finding out things by accident, of being ignored. Geraldine allows herself the luxury of standing up, not caring who sees her. She slips into the seat next door to Gerald.

'Why didn't you tell me you'd got into the orchestra?' she demands. 'I've been trying to find out for months and months. No one tells me *anything*.'

Gerald, like the conductor earlier, just looks at her. No surprise, just a faint smile.

'I thought it must be you.'

'You knew?'

'Oh yes. But you weren't doing anyone any harm. Quiet as a mouse.'

Ha!

'And I daresay you enjoyed feeling almost part of the orchestra?' He smiles, then his expression changes. 'Geraldine, I hesitate to say this, but won't your mother be wondering where you are?'

'Mr Gerald. You haven't answered my question.'

'Geraldine, I only started this week. I didn't know myself until recently. I had another audition.'

'What happened the first time?'

'It wasn't too good. Rusty. But they said to re-audition in three months, which I did.'

'That was mean.'

'No, they were right. Technique, confidence – they're coming back, slowly. Of course I know the *Nutcracker* well enough. I suppose,' he says pointedly, 'you wanted to watch our famous lady conductor in action. She's good, isn't she?'

But Geraldine is in no mood for talking about that. They are almost the only two people left in the pit.

'I'd better go.'

'Yes, you should. Do you want me to come with you?'

'No.' Some things are better faced alone. Besides, this is something between herself and her mother.

In the end, though, she does not face the music alone. She is just about to climb up onto a chair to get out of the pit when she hears a voice.

'Jellybean. How *could* you?' It's Mum, stooping through the pit door, hands on hips.

'You realize I've missed the whole of the second act because of you.'

'Yes.'

'And I've been worrying myself sick outside in that miserable cold arcade for over an hour. Walking up and down Queen Street.'

'Mmm.'

'And if Frederica hadn't come out just now and told me where you were, I would have gone off to the police station.'

'Mmm. Who's Frederica?'

'The conductor, you know. She said she saw you right in the corner of the pit, behind the celeste.'

'How does she know me?'

'She's a smart lady. Put two and two together, didn't she? *And* took the trouble to come and find me.'

This low urgent voice – because there are still dancers and managers talking on the stage above – is almost worse than the anger Geraldine had expected. Gerald is quietly sorting out music, pretending not to hear anything. When Geraldine fails to respond, her mother heaves an enormous sigh and begins to pack away her cello.

'*Jellybean* . . .'

'Don't call me that.'

'Just don't ever do that to me again, Jellybean.'

'*Don't* call . . .'

'All right. Geraldine. Just don't. . .'

Her voice trails off in a most un-Mum-like manner. Geraldine looks sharply at the seated figure. Her mother is absent-mindedly unscrewing the cello bow. Even with her face in profile, Geraldine can see the wetness in her eyes.

She longs to comfort her mother and to be comforted. She just cannot take the first step. So she stands, feeling stupid, and stares up at the remaining dancers who are repeating a movement while the ballet master pom-poms the music and watches critically.

It is Gerald who moves and puts a hand on her mother's shoulder.

'It's all right, Anna. Nothing happened, you know that.'

Her mother wipes her hand across her eyes, as though angry with herself.

'I've been through the whole gamut of what could have happened: car accident, run over by a bus, abduction, rape, kidnapping, lost, gone down to the ferry buildings and fallen in the water, electrocuted backstage. God knows there are enough wires around the place. . .'

'Anna. Forget all that.'

Her mother nods.

Geraldine stiffens. What is going on? For someone who joined the orchestra only last week, Gerald seems to know her mother very well, nicknames and all. The morning has proved quite exhausting enough, thank you very much. All she wants to do now is go home and read a book.

'Let's go,' Geraldine says very quietly, almost to herself. And amazingly, they do just that, with very little more talk, leaving Gerald standing alone with his cello at the entrance to the arcade, looking after them.

12

The ballet opens the following night, a Thursday. For Geraldine, two weeks of baby-sitters lie ahead and for the first time, the prospect annoys her. The dress rehearsal, unsettling as it was, has given her a taste for backstage. She seriously considers asking her mother to get her some sort of job, as a messenger, anything, so that she can go with her each night to the theatre.

The reaction would be predictable: too late, too tired for school the next day, they don't want people hanging about backstage, and, what could you do? Nothing, she would have to reply.

So she is kissed goodbye, sharp on seven on Thursday night, feeling a mixture of resentment and resignation. 'I'm going a bit early tonight,' her mother explains cheerfully to Veronica, the babysitter. 'Yesterday I cut it a bit fine.' Veronica is standing in the kitchen with a pile of music. Geraldine knows that the instant the Mini backs out the drive, the piano will burst into sound. Three hours of boring music, and worse, endless scales, lie ahead.

Shutting her bedroom door on the arpeggios, Geraldine lies on her bed, imagining the theatre. Her mother and Gerald will be tuning up in the pit, while backstage Susie is getting ready (she couldn't imagine Susie ever getting nervous about anything) and Mrs Taylor is fussing round her stuck-up Jenny. Dressing-rooms will be full of party guests, soldiers, dolls, mice, snowflakes, other children. In the arcade those iron gates will be unlocked and the audience gathering – excited children on early Christmas treats shouted by their grandparents. Eventually she sleeps, with dreams of mice. Then somehow she has got hold of a white stick and is conducting an orchestra so vast that she can't even see the players in the rear seats. They all have their instruments ready; they and she begin a beautiful waltz but the sound gradually turns to a mocking laughter, even though they are all still playing . . .

I'm real, she decides, the street light shining through the crack in the curtains is real, Quaver sleeping on the end of my bed is real, and so is *some* sort of music and the laughter. It is her mother's laugh, she realizes, among others . . .

Cautiously she pads down the hallway, taking care not to step on any boards that squeak, towards the half open door. The studio is in shadows, lit only by an orange glow coming from the gas fire, but there is enough light to see first the cello, upright and black in the corner, and then two heads near the fireplace. Immediately Geraldine feels an outsider. In her own home, it is not an experience she enjoys.

The murmured conversation blends with the background of a string quartet, creating an atmosphere of such intimacy that Geraldine shivers. She cannot quite hear the words that are being said; maybe her own name more than once, although she cannot be sure. Made reckless with frustration, she suddenly has to back into the corner behind the door when her mother gets up and walks over to the dresser.

'. . . a brandy, to celebrate your return,' she says. 'Four years is a long time away.'

'You can't imagine how I've missed it.' The voice, raised a little, comes clearly to Geraldine's ears behind the door. 'There were times, catching the tube night after night to Covent Garden, through slush and rain, when I'd willingly have given it all away. But when the choice is taken away from you. . .'

So it is Gerald in there. Groups of musicians she is used

to; single women, gossiping over a bottle of wine, she is used to. Single men, drinking brandy and talking late into the night with her mother, she is *not* used to.

She hears the bottle being replaced on the dresser, and footsteps as her mother returns to the fireplace. 'To London,' her mother says clearly. 'To memories.' Geraldine, peeping around the door, sees them touch glasses, big balloon glasses glowing bronze in the firelight. 'What a time that was . . . I shall never forget that night at the Royal Albert Hall, Beecham conducting, September of that first year. Remember? We weren't up in the gods, but in a very expensive box, some free tickets we'd been given.'

Geraldine pulls back and almost runs up the hallway to her bedroom. '*Remember*?' She quietly closes the door, turns on her bedside light and tries to read, but the word keeps pushing itself between her mind and the print. So they knew each other all along. Why didn't they tell her?

'You went to sleep with your light on, Jellybean,' says her mother cheerfully, pulling back the curtains.

Geraldine knows she does not want to wake up, but it takes her a few moments to remember why she has this sinking feeling in her stomach.

'Terrific opening night last night. I really enjoyed it. That little Clara is a pet. The audience loved her. Susan Stevens her name is. They say she's going to go a long way.'

Getting no response, she sits on the bed.

'Let's see what the paper says. Here. "Clara was danced by Susan Stevens with great charm and style." I bet they don't mention the orchestra. We'll get one line at the end if we're lucky. Well, well. Half-way through, no less. "Musically, the evening exceeded expectations, with the orchestra in top form under the capable baton of Frederica Wilton making her debut as a ballet conductor. Already a noted pianist and director of musical comedy, Ms Wilton gave clear evidence of her growing stature as one of the most versatile musicians produced in this country. She directed both orchestra and dancers with sensitivity and grace." Isn't it wonderful! I'm so pleased for her. There were two or three men in the orchestra who almost refused to play under a woman conductor. That'll silence them.'

'I thought she was only doing the matinees,' mumbles Geraldine.

'Maestro has 'flu, usual spring epidemic.' She looks up from the paper. 'How did you know that?'

Under the duvet, Geraldine shrugs.

Her mother leans over to stroke Geraldine's cheek. Geraldine turns away. 'Anything wrong?'

'I feel sick.' Not sick sick, just sick of . . . feeling a nobody.

'Well, you'd better stay there. I've nothing on today, at all. Just the ballet tonight. Leanne's coming to baby-sit.'

Geraldine grunts. Her mother is uncommonly cheerful this morning.

'You kept me awake last night.'

'Sorry, little one. I had a couple of friends back after the show. We talked rather late.'

'A couple?'

Her mother looks at her sharply, but Geraldine's eyes are closed, giving nothing away.

'Hey, Jellybean. I've got a couple of tickets for the ballet matinee on Saturday, very good tickets, front row of the circle. Would you like to ask a friend?'

'I don't have any friends.' Only Susie, and she's dancing.

Short silence. 'Well, think about it.'

'I'd like to go with you,' says Geraldine firmly.

A long silence this time.

'With me? But . . .'

'Yes.'

'Well, I suppose . . . I suppose I can get someone to

sit in for me. Someone will have to take my place. You need a certain number of cellos. People can't just drop out, you know.'

Then, with more conviction, she adds, 'Okay, I'll see what I can do. Jessie, possibly, or Pat might fill in for me.'

Geraldine is astonished. What has happened, that her mother should forego the orchestra just to take her, Geraldine, to a show? She decides she might get up after all.

So, for the first time, on Saturday afternoon, all dressed up, they go to the ballet together. Her mother is loudly hailed by some of the players, immaculate in black evening dress, going in by the stage door. Instead of her usual embarrassment, Geraldine is pleased by the looks other children give her mother. They walk up the marble staircase just like anyone else, and find their seats in the very front of the circle.

Together they watch the orchestra assembling in the pit. Gerald is one of the first to arrive. With himself, cello, and music organized, he looks up searchingly at the circle. Geraldine cannot tell whether that shy smile is for her or her mother, or both. Her mother waves back, rather too obviously for Geraldine's liking. Geraldine hopes he notices that she is actually far more interested in the harp player.

The lights dim and the many children in the audience gasp with anticipation. Then the tall figure of Frederica in a slim-fitting black dress appears from the side of the auditorium and takes a jaunty bow. Geraldine and her mother clap as loudly as they can. They clap every dance, from start to finish, filling in the deathly hush of the dress rehearsal.

Susie is wonderful, and even Jenny can dance, Geraldine has to admit. The squabble over the Nutcracker again moves her to tears. She is properly repelled by the Mouse King and the fearful music of the battle dream. The transformation from the big party room with its sofas and chandeliers and outsize Christmas tree of Clara's dream to the Pine Forest in the Land of Snow is pure magic. And if it wasn't for the delicate flute waltz and the women's voices offstage singing that long sweet melody she might indeed have agreed with Susie about 'all those snowflakes.'

The interval, mostly spent queuing for an ice-cream from the small shop by the stage along with every other child from the audience, seems like an eternity. When the conductor returns for the second act, she gets a spontaneous extra clap, even some cheers, which prompt her to make all the orchestra rise to share the applause. Geraldine claps until her hands are sore.

How the second act flashes by now that she can see the whole stage properly and simply absorb the familiar music and marvel at that person who is thirty and female and controlling it all. The grandeur of the final pas de deux music once again arouses that impossible yearning – for what she does not know. The celeste, since she cannot dissociate it from the unknown Gerald in the pit, has acquired a cutting edge, and she is glad when its part is over and the dancers swing into the final waltz.

All too soon the lights fade. To the exquisite bell music of the final few bars the scene miraculously dissolves into the big party room of the first act with the sleeping Susie at the back of the stage.

Geraldine claps until she can clap no more. It is one of the best afternoons of her life.

Until, that is, they walk back down the marble staircase and stop outside the stage door. Geraldine stands apart while her mother greets various friends emerging with their instrument cases. 'Wonderful show,' she says. 'I'm so glad Geraldine bullied me into taking her. Marvellous to see it out front.' Not fair and not true, Mum, protests Geraldine silently. Don't spoil it for me.

But the afternoon is spoilt as Gerald now joins the group.

There is no escaping her mother's outstretched hand and worse, her invitation to 'Meet an old friend', followed by his boring polite questions about did you enjoy the show.

Whose old friend?

'We met once before, at a rehearsal, some months ago,' Gerald is saying. 'Oh yes, so you did,' says her mother. Geraldine cannot meet their eyes. To her profound relief he does not mention women conductors, or make any reference to the dress rehearsal. She would have *died* if he had.

Not a minute too soon they are walking back to the car. For once, Geraldine sits in the front seat. Inside her, two sets of emotions are whirling about and colliding. To think of the perfection of the dancing and the music makes her feel all tingly and good; to think of Gerald fills her with a vague dread. And since her mother makes no further reference to him – whose old friend? – she decides she won't either. She simply will not bother to ask. It's a decision which somehow gives her considerable satisfaction. It is, after all, her only weapon.

13

Back at school on Monday, sitting in an assembly which seems to go on for ever, she is dismayed to hear that her yearly ordeal is coming around again. She has given up reading the schedule by the telephone. 'People,' the headmaster is saying, 'I'm very pleased to tell you that the orchestra will be coming next week to give us a wonderful programme of music.'

Sure – 'Star Wars' and T.V. themes and the 'Toy Symphony' again, thinks Geraldine with scorn. And always some clever dick in her class says before school, 'Your mother's coming, isn't she? To play her cello.' Almost as though it was her fault. How they found out Geraldine has no idea, since she certainly never told anyone at school about anything. Then, a gushing teacher stands up before her class and informs everyone that 'we are lucky to have Geraldine in our class because Geraldine's mother plays in the orchestra we're going to hear today and isn't she lucky to have such a talented mother?' – or words to that effect.

Worst of all, as the orchestra arrives on the dreaded morning, 'Which is your Mum, Geraldine?' and 'That's her, with all the hair, and the funny clothes,' comes from some other busybody short on tact. Her mother waves from her seat, not a big Hi-it's-me wave, but enough, oh yes, enough.

'I've got a stomach ache,' she announces when the morning finally arrives. 'I think I'll stay home.'

'Not today. No,' replies her mother with unusual speed. Then, 'What sort of stomach ache?'

'All over. Here,' she rubs her tummy.

'You know I'm playing today. At your school.'

'So you'll be home by lunchtime. And,' Geraldine adds triumphantly (having checked the calendar by the telephone), 'you've nothing on this afternoon. I'll be all right.'

'No, sorry. You're not old enough for that yet. Even for a morning. Sorry, Jellybean. You're just going to have to take an aspirin and come.'

'Oh, Mum . . .'

'You haven't had a stomach ache in years,' her mother says, just a little accusingly.

'Well, I have now.'

'An aspirin will fix it. You'll just be sitting. And you can come home with me at lunchtime if it's not better by then.'

Geraldine knows that tone of voice when she hears it. She speaks as little as possible through breakfast and doing dishes and driving to school. As soon as the car is parked, she leaps out and leaves mother with cello to make her own way into the school hall. And it gives her almost a real ache in her heart to see from a distance her mother walk slowly down the drive and into the school hall – with Gerald, both of them carrying their cellos. Why does she feel so full of hurt? His memory rubs at her like a stone inside a sneaker.

The classes file into the hall and sit on the floor. Around the walls sit the teachers and some extra mothers, the non-working variety; those, thinks Geraldine sourly, who could allow their child to spend a day at home with a stomach ache. The orchestra is nearly ready. Dully, ignoring the usual comments about Mum, that's her with the hair, Geraldine watches the familiar faces, the familiar preparation and the chat between the players.

She notices, with some surprise, that there is a woman seated at a small keyboard instrument. It can only be her old friend the celeste, now seen for the first time in broad daylight. Does that mean there will be some music from the *Nutcracker*?

There is one other positive aspect to the day. While the headmaster does his long-winded thing introducing the orchestra, Geraldine notices the tall figure standing quietly by the wall.

'I'll hand over now, to the orchestra's conductor, Frederica Wilton.'

The school claps, politely. She walks over to the rostrum, smiles and bows. Seeing her now also for the first time in daylight, Geraldine decides that she is altogether more attractive than she first thought: smartly dressed, dark, and that clever face.

Not only can she conduct; it becomes apparent that she can talk as well. Geraldine finds her interest being held as Frederica introduces each piece, making even 'Star Wars' sound interesting. Finally comes the 'Toy Symphony'. A hall full of eager hands goes up when she calls for volunteers to conduct. A small boy, about J Two size, gets picked. There is the usual carry-on showing him how to beat time, and more when various teachers are asked to come and play the percussion toy drums and whistles and cuckoos and things. Frederica makes it all seem like a great adventure, and even Geraldine finds herself enjoying it as much as the rest of the school.

When all the laughter and clapping has died away, Geraldine waits for the headmaster to come forward and say his thank you piece. Instead, it is clear that Frederica has something more to say.

'Today we've something a little special for you. Usually when we go to schools, we finish with the 'Toy Symphony' because all the players are exhausted.' Behind her the players look out at the school and smile.

'I expect quite a few of you went during the holidays

to the ballet *Casse Noisette*. Is that right?' Hands go up all over the hall.

'Terrific. So many of you will have heard Tchaikovsky's wonderful music and will know the next two pieces we are going to play.'

'Sugar Plum Fairy', no doubt, thinks Geraldine, brightening. She sees Gerald looking at her.

There is an expectant pause while Frederica looks down at her feet deep in thought. Finally she looks up and continues.

'Today we're going to have a rather special conductor. I'm not asking for volunteers, although I know many of you would love to have the opportunity to conduct a fine orchestra like this. It's a great privilege, believe me. Instead, I'm going to ask a young lady who knows this music rather better than most of you.'

What is she saying?

'This young lady is quite well known to the orchestra. She has had to spend many hours of her young life attending rehearsals, since she was only as big as some of you in the front rows.' She smiles down at the five-year-olds.

A dreadful suspicion is forming in Geraldine's mind.

'Perhaps you can imagine . . .' She pauses and looks around at the hushed hall. 'If you sat through many many rehearsals, you might quite naturally wonder what it would be like to conduct an orchestra.'

Geraldine is beginning to feel very hot.

'So I'm going to ask Geraldine Waite to come forward and conduct these two pieces from *Casse Noisette*.'

The school shuffles. People in front turn around. Teachers' heads are turned towards her.

'Geraldine?' Frederica's eyes are searching the hall. And since Geraldine does not – cannot – immediately move, the call comes again. 'Geraldine?'

Elbows ram into her sides. 'Go on, silly.' There is an undercurrent of whispers around the hall.

Still she cannot move. She is too shocked to move. She dare not look at her mother. Then her eyes meet Gerald's and she knows it is a put-up job. That is why her mother wouldn't let her stay away from school. Gerald is smiling encouragement and nodding his head slightly.

She wishes the polished cork tiles would split apart and swallow her up. She wants to stagger to her feet, rush out the back of the hall and not stop running until she reaches the end of the world.

Frederica is walking down the side aisle between the children and teachers, to the back of the hall. She is holding out her hand. Escape is hopeless.

Geraldine climbs slowly to her feet and picks her way to the end of the row between knees and black school shoes. Frederica takes her hand and leads her to her doom. The whispers have now become an excited murmur and swell into clapping.

She is lead to the rostrum, the white stick is put into her hand. She cannot bring herself to look at either her mother or Gerald. Traitors.

She looks helplessly at the score in front of her. 'Dance of the Sugar Plum Fairy'. It is nothing like her piano music, nor her mother's cello music, just a dense mass of closely printed lines and notes over every page. Panic is now rising fast.

Behind her there is still the murmur of four hundred children. She knows she is bright scarlet, all over. Soon they will begin laughing . . .

'Geraldine, just relax and enjoy it,' says a low voice beside her. 'Now, you know the dance of the "Sugar Plum Fairy", don't you?'

She nods, still too shocked to speak.

'Okay. Now.' Frederica turns back to address the

audience which immediately falls silent. 'Now that Geraldine is getting over her surprise, here are two pieces from the *Nutcracker* ballet.' And she launches into the story about Tchaikovsky and his secret celeste that once, years ago it seems, Gerald had told her.

Holding the baton, Geraldine looks around the orchestra. Their familiar faces now seem melted together into an ocean of eyes. She feels like a lighthouse. Then she forces herself to look over to the cellos. Her mother's face is unreadable behind her cupped hand. Gerald's is rather more interesting. He is nodding quite noticeably now, and on his lips she clearly reads 'Good, good.' His eyes are like beacons, willing her on.

Whatever Frederica has said leaves the audience laughing as she turns back to Geraldine. 'Now, we'll do this together,' she says quietly, coming and standing directly behind her.

'Can I . . . Can I . . . just . . . by myself?' says Geraldine.

There might have been a slight hesitation, but she says. 'Why not? Get the tempo in your head. It's all yours.'

Frederica draws back out of sight. Geraldine is left alone on the podium. She raises her two arms. The players lift their instruments, look at her, dead serious. She holds it in her two hands – that magical moment of anticipation before the music begins.

The white baton moves. The opening four bars of the accompaniment are plucked, very soft, then the celeste begins its icy tune. Geraldine forgets all the hundreds of eyes behind her. She hears only the music which now she is playing. She seems to know by instinct when to bring the celeste player in; their eyes meet across the music stands. She realizes too that the players are watching her a lot more closely than is apparent to an audience.

The ending throws her a bit, as the players use the longer ending she noticed in the theatre, not the shorter one she has grown used to on the tape. But how the music ripples and dances to its conclusion. One joyful pizzicato chord and it is over. Amazingly, there is clapping behind her.

'Take a bow,' says a voice. She does and . . . wow! What an incredible feeling. Then she remembers that the celeste player has done all the work, so she extends her arm, just as she has always seen conductors do towards their soloists, and makes the smiling player stand and take a bow too. Geraldine dares not smile, for fear that once her face cracked she would begin to laugh for pure joy.

So she stands solemnly, keeping her eyes well away from the cello section, while Frederica introduces the 'Waltz of the Flowers' and they are off again. The beginning is complicated, with a long harp solo, but the players seem to have everything under control and soon they are swinging into that glorious waltz. Towards the end she feels like speeding up a little, so she does, and the players follow her to a slightly breathless conclusion. She is exhilarated, as though she has just climbed a mountain or danced the whole waltz herself through a ballroom of mirrors and candles.

Through the clapping, which is louder again, Frederica says, 'What about the "Russian Dance" as an encore?'

'Yes. Please.'

'Dum, diddle dum dum, dum dum DUM,' Frederica hums. 'You know it. Not too fast.'

Around her the 'Russian dance' bounces along. At the end she gets somewhat carried away and speeds up too much for the players as it turns out, for when the music finishes they put down their instruments with relief and a collective expression of 'phew' on their faces.

The audience roars with laughter, the orchestra grins, and the clapping is loud and warm.

As they stand together, acknowledging the applause, Frederica says 'Well done, kid.'

'That was a bit fast, wasn't it?'

'A bit. Do them good. Keeps them on their toes.'

The clapping is still going on. There are even some cheers from the back of the hall.

'Would you like one last piece? What about the "Grand Pas de deux" from the Second Act. You know it.'

Her heart sinks. 'Not . . . not really.'

'You heard it the other day from your rather unusual place,' she says, her eyes smiling. 'The first dance of the Sugar Plum Fairy and her Prince. Very slow, very loud, majestic stuff. Fabulous.'

'I'm not sure . . .'

'You'll be okay. Steady four-four time. You'll find they'll just keep going, whatever you do.' Now the clapping is diminishing. 'Okay?'

For a moment Geraldine feels quite dashed. So they don't really need a conductor at all. The orchestra just gets going and they play on, regardless.

'No, I . . .'

But the impetus is too great for Geraldine to stop, because Frederica has turned to the orchestra and quietly said 'Intrada, Pas de Deux, Act Two' and is now talking to the hall, telling them about the Sugar Plum Fairy and her Prince who do this wonderful love duet. Geraldine stands unhappily waiting. She steals a look at Gerald and is again cheered by the encouragement in his eyes. He even mimes a small clap.

'We'll do this together, okay?' says Frederica right behind her. Geraldine gratefully accepts the offer of a hand to guide the baton through the opening bars. The harp is the first to respond. Now she recognizes the music and it is everything Frederica has said: soaring sounds which fill the whole hall and towards the dance's mighty end threaten to carry Geraldine away completely. Again she feels that shiver which starts at the back of her skull as the music builds up and engulfs her. Then there's a brief passage of a downward wistful quality, soft and sad, before the final climax, timpani, trumpets, everything, which finally shoots her quivering into space.

Then silence, before the school erupts into applause.

Geraldine looks across at the cellos. Her mother is grinning broadly and behind her Gerald is leaning back in his chair and clapping. In a daze she hears a voice telling her to take a bow. She remembers to get the orchestra to stand and take theirs, too. Frederica bows beside her. After the second bow Geraldine can go on no longer. She sits down heavily on the rostrum and looks at her feet. When the clapping finally dies away, the headmaster comes and says his final piece. Geraldine hears only the sound of his voice, not a single word.

The concert is over. A hum of excited conversation breaks out. The orchestra players stand and start packing up their instruments. Geraldine feels like a balloon that has been popped. And as the reality of what she has done sinks in, she begins to tremble all over. It starts at her neck. Before it goes any further, she knows she has to get away, out, away.

Frederica is just sitting down beside her on the rostrum and the headmaster is walking over towards her, when she springs to her feet. Looking neither right nor left, she walks away from the rostrum, away from the cello section, away from all the teachers and the staring J Ones in the front rows, away from the hall and away from the school.

14

While passing the windows of the school hall Geraldine walks slowly, with great dignity. Before she is half-way up the drive she is jogging. Out of the school gates she is running. Along the road she hurtles.

It is her frequent dream: running but never getting any further away from the unidentified fear behind her. All those eyes . . . looking! When she begins to slow down, she finds that her legs have taken her in the direction of the playground and the green terraced hill rising behind it.

The urge to push herself to the brink of exhaustion is so strong that before long she is clambering towards the top, between groups of staring lambs and their mothers.

Mothers! How *could* her own mother spring that on her? And Gerald? Worse again. He was the only person in the whole world who knew about her ambition to conduct an orchestra, and only he could have betrayed her. He must have told her mother, and the whole orchestra. She climbs on relentlessly. Why? Why?

Her whole body is aching when she reaches the top. Ignoring the few sightseers walking around the obelisk, she sits panting against the trunk of the one tree. Like the tree, she feels totally alone. Funny place to hide, she thinks, yet somehow the vastness of the scene below her is strangely soothing. No one would think of looking for her up here. Her mind is as empty as a seabird flying over one of those far distant islands.

Soon she begins to feel chilled. The skies above the city are low and grey and her school sweatshirt is not much protection against the spring wind. After a while she has to get up and walk around. She hugs herself to keep warm. How is it possible to feel so alone? Clapped and cheered by the whole school half an hour ago, she now wishes she were dead. Tears of pity, for herself and the friend she has lost in Gerald, blur the grey clouds.

Of course, Mum will be looking for her. Well, let her. But Geraldine is beginning to feel a little foolish. She can't stay up here all day. Sooner or later they will have to be faced. There is one other refuge and that is her room. There she can shut the door on her mother and anyone else she feels like, and stroke Quaver, her only true friend.

She follows the road down from the stone ramparts on the summit. Soon she finds herself skipping, then running down through a broad paddock, feeling oddly light-headed. She skips and swoops and does the occasional ballerina-like long jump across ditches and even over a sleeping sheep. Once she stumbles on the knobbly grass and a pain shoots through her ankle, but she runs on and down.

A great sense of space and freedom has taken hold of her. Now she knows. I did it, she laughs, taking a mighty leap into the air. I've been a conductor! No one can take that away from me, ever.

Trees close in around her, some tipped with the first green of spring. She climbs over stiles, crosses the road again. And as she descends from the heights she finds her pace is slowing, and her mood of elation sinking. By the time she approaches the playground it has worn off almost completely.

It isn't fair, she cries silently as she walks around the flying fox and the high wooden towers, in no mood to try any of them. My life was doing okay until Gerald came along. Nothing has been quite the same since then.

Apart from a young mother with a fat baby in a push-chair eating their lonely lunch at one of the picnic tables, the playground is deserted. None of the usual things appeal:

the cargo net, or the big tube of wooden slats which swings ten feet above the ground, or the fireman's pole. They are no fun, alone. Only the ordinary old swing suits her mood, facing down towards the entrance from the main road.

She has been swinging quietly for a few minutes, trying to make a blank of her mind, when she notices a solitary car drive into the car park and a figure appear. It is not the person she would have chosen to force her re-entry into the real world. She stops the swing and turns the other way, presenting her back. She feels an urge to get up and run, but a stronger urge holds her on the swing. Perhaps now she will find out some answers.

She swings high, pulling hard on her arms, strongly up and up. Out of the corner of her eye, she sees Gerald sit down on the swing beside her and start to move gently back and forth. He knows, of course, that I can't keep this up for ever, she thinks angrily. But she tries, oh how she tries, until her arms are aching and she is beginning to feel more than a little seasick. Eventually her swing hangs nearly still.

She refuses to look at him. Instead she stares at the summit of the hill with its silver needle obelisk and single tree.

'We were *so* proud of you,' he begins. 'You have a great feeling for music.'

'Who's we?'

'Your mother . . . and me.'

'It was horrible. I hated it.'

'Did you?' Gently spoken, but pointed. He knew it wasn't true. 'My humble impression was that you really enjoyed your experience this morning. You did a *very* good job. As a debut it was more than promising.'

'I tell you, I hated every single minute. It wasn't fair.'

'No, maybe not,' he concedes.

'To spring that on me, in front of the whole school.

And it must have been you. I never told anyone else.' She turns to look at him accusingly.'You told *everybody*,' she continues. 'It's all right for people to go around saying they want to be nurses or doctors or ballet dancers or computer programmers, but no one says they want to be conductors.'

'Why not? It seems a very praiseworthy ambition to me. A very difficult one, but admirable.'

What was the use? But before she can protest further, Gerald continues, 'Geraldine. Yes, I did tell your mother of your great joy in music. I don't think she quite recognized how intense your feeling was. To give you the opportunity to conduct, she had to know. And yes, the orchestra's manager had to give permission. But no one else knew. The other players? Certainly not. It wasn't necessary for them to know any more than . . . Well, it was just a nice opportunity to do something a little different, a surprise for your school.'

'Why did you have to tell Mum? Why? Why couldn't it stay just our secret?'

During the long silence Geraldine is conscious of a baby's cry. She looks around and is dismayed to see the mother in the playground lashing out, smacking the child once, twice, three times on the hand. Since she has never been smacked on the hand or anywhere else, the sight of young mothers hitting their children in public upsets her.

Gerald follows her glance and obviously notices her expression of disgust.

'When you've no children of your own, that's hard to understand or condone,' he says.

'My mother has never smacked me, ever,' says Geraldine stiffly. 'She doesn't believe in it. I think it's awful.'

He nods. She has the impression that he is trying to say something, and finding it difficult to start.

'Geraldine. I . . . I have to tell you something.'

No, she cries silently, don't tell me you're my father. After what has just happened, she doesn't want that. Yet it is true that she has dreamed of a stranger who one day would appear out of the blue and claim her. She waits fearfully.

When he cannot go on, she finds the silence intolerable.

She says, lifting her chin, 'I've never known what my father looked like. I don't want to know.'

Out of the corner of her eye she sees his head turn slightly, as though surprised. Then he smiles a little.

'Geraldine, that isn't what I had to tell you.'

Part of her cries out with relief and collides with another feeling which cries in sorrow.

'But I do know your father. If you want me to, I can tell you about him.'

'No. Anyway, how do you know him?'

'Do you know nothing at all about him?'

'Not much,' she shrugs, trying to appear nonchalant. 'Just . . . that he played the viola. And he went off before I was even born. I don't know where to. Mum has never told me. Perhaps she doesn't know herself.'

'She does now. I told her. He married again and has two children. He has been playing for some years in the Orchestra of the Royal Opera House, Covent Garden.'

Geraldine turns and looks at him sharply.

'With . . .? One thing Geraldine knows and that is that orchestra players get to know each other well.

'Yes.'

'Why are you telling me all this?'

'There's . . . There's more.'

Down to the nitty-gritty, she thinks.

'I think you . . . have realized that your mother and I knew each other well. A long time ago.'

'No.' But she did, now that it was put into words.

'During her two student years in London we saw a lot

of each other. We were both students, working hard, our lives totally immersed in music. They were two wonderful years for both of us. Half-way through, we agreed to marry.'

'So what happened?' says Geraldine, absorbed despite herself.

'I don't know. Things just started to go wrong, towards the end of her second year. She wanted to come back here. I wasn't ready to come out to what I thought was a country a long way from the musical centre of things. I couldn't believe that there was an orchestra and a musical life to be had here that would satisfy me.'

'That wasn't right, was it?'

'No. So . . . she came home, she met your father and married him within weeks. The next thing, you were on the way. Your father . . . while your mother was carrying you, he fell in love with someone else. . .'

'In the orchestra?'

'I believe so, yes. And that was the end of the marriage.'

'Why has my mother never told me all this?'

'Perhaps the opportunity or the need has never arisen. Perhaps she thought you weren't quite old enough.'

The baby has stopped crying now, Geraldine notes. There is even a weak sun trying to break through the grey roof of clouds, catching the silver pointer on the summit.

'The rest . . . about my wife dying, my years of living up north, and trying to get back into music . . . you know.'

'That's why you came to the restaurant that night . . . to . . .'

'Renew a friendship that once meant a great deal to me. Yes,' he smiles. 'To meet the child who was named after me. Yes. But, as you probably realized, I got cold feet that night. And again before my audition. I didn't make proper contact with your mother until a few days after the audition.'

It is almost too much for Geraldine to take in. So he could almost have been my father . . . but then I wouldn't be who I am now, I'd be someone else.

A nasty thought strikes her, hard.

'You're not going to marry my mother, are you?' Geraldine has had enough for one day.

'No.' She hears the slightest of chuckles. 'No, Geraldine, you and she have your life together. For the moment, the more important thing is our friendship, nothing more nor less. In the fullness of time . . . who knows. Things change. No one can see what lies ahead.'

I can, thinks Geraldine. Looking her mother in the eye will be difficult. As for school tomorrow, the very thought makes her shudder. Yet she is feeling a great sense of relief. Things were not going to be much changed, just better. She begins to swing higher and higher, pulling back hard on her arms to gain height. Beside her Gerald follows, less vigorously.

She shouts, 'Does Mum know you're telling me all this?'

'Yes. It was her idea. Actually, she's waiting over in the car.'

Geraldine sees now that there is a head in the front seat of his car. She allows the swing to subside a little, and readies herself for a final grand leap off from the top of the arc. Landing heavily, she rolls over and over on the grass. Gerald does a much smaller leap off and runs until the impetus of his jump is spent. She realizes that his run is the run of a much younger man than his greying beard had led her to believe. She notices that he is wearing running shoes and jeans and a smart leather jacket. Nothing moth-eaten about him at all, she decides.

'Shall we go and meet her?' he says.

But her mother has already climbed out of the car and is walking across the grass towards them. They come together and stop. Geraldine looks at her feet.

'I've been thinking, Gerald,' her mother begins. 'Jellybean has her eleventh birthday in January. I have some money saved up, not a vast sum, but enough for one and a half airfares to London and back. Enough to get a small loan from my friendly neighbourhood bank manager. If I take on a few pupils next year I can pay it off comfortably. You wouldn't mind that, Jellybean, in the afternoons? I'd be at home.'

Jellybean looks up, incredulous. She has never seen her mother's eyes sparkle so, far more than they ever did with nerves before a concert.

'We could leave just before Christmas, when the orchestra goes into summer recess. It's what, September now . . . Mmm . . . probably not too late to book for a pre-Christmas flight. And the travel agent can tell us how to get good seats for a birthday treat at Covent Garden.'

The silence positively sings.

'Are you saying . . . to *England*?' says Geraldine eventually.

'Yes.'

'Go to Covent Garden? To see a ballet?'

'Or opera. Depends on what's on. Yes, well, it's a good excuse. I've got lots of friends to see in London. We can stay with Angela. Remember her Gerald? She was studying viola. She got married, stayed on, does freelance work with quite a few of the big orchestras.

'And we can get to a concert or two at the Albert Hall and the Festival Hall, and perhaps some rehearsals if Angela can arrange it. And the Changing of the Guard and all the usual things. And of course we'll have to make contact with Jonathan.' Her voice falters slightly and Geraldine sees her look sideways at Gerald. 'But I can cope with that now and I expect he'll want to meet his musical daughter. He might even be able to arrange for us to see a rehearsal at Covent Garden. I don't know if that's allowed, but it's worth a go.'

Gerald breaks the silence left after this torrent of words.

'Jonathan,' he says gently to Geraldine, 'is your . . .'

Geraldine, reeling, nods. Then she says, 'Couldn't you come with us? Couldn't he, Mum? To London?'

Neither of them answers immediately, but Geraldine knows from the smile under Gerald's beard that he can come, and will.

'Well, money-wise, I could just about . . .'

'Good, that's all settled then,' says her mother briskly.

'Shouldn't we perhaps talk about it a little more deeply, Anna. You may want to . . .'

'Why?'

'Well. You and Geraldine may want to discuss it first.'

For an answer her mother takes a step, holds his head with both hands, and kisses him briefly on the mouth. Then she takes Geraldine's hand and starts to walk down the hill.

'I've also been thinking, Gerald,' she says, 'that it's about time Jellybean began to learn something. Other than the piano, which I don't think satisfies her greatly.'

Geraldine smiles at the grass.

'Do you have any preferences, Jellybean? I don't want to assume that the cello would necessarily be your first choice, just because of us.'

Suddenly Geraldine feels as light-headed as she had when leaping and skipping down the mountain. The cello will be her first choice and Gerald her teacher, but she's not going to say that, just yet.

'The celeste,' she says wickedly.